# ALOHA!

Stephen A. Enna & Dennis J. Wootten

authorHOUSE®

AuthorHouse™
1663 Liberty Drive
Bloomington, IN 47403
www.authorhouse.com
Phone: 1-800-839-8640

First published by AuthorHouse    05/11/2011

ISBN: 978-1-4567-5196-8 (e)
ISBN: 978-1-4567-5197-5 (hc)
ISBN: 978-1-4567-5198-2 (sc)

Library of Congress Control Number: 2011903697

Printed in the United States of America

"Aloha" is the first book of our political trilogy. Watch for the second book, "Adios" and the third book, "Goodbye" in the coming months.

We dedicate "Aloha" to our wives, family, friends and employees. Their comments, edits, and constructive criticism proved invaluable.

Thanks to all of you!

Den & Steve

# ALOHA!

## THE PROLOGUE

**Portland, Oregon
2013**

It was 11 PM, smoke filled the air in the cigar bar just off Broadway in downtown Portland. The Oregon rain was pelting the Pearl District Streets as though God had decided it needed a thorough cleaning. It was July. Normally July is a dry month in Oregon. Not this July. There was no humidity, just constant rain. Jesus, he thought, *it just never stops in this town*. Who would have predicted that this long-time skid row district would become the center of the art community and the hotbed of liberal activism in Oregon?

It had only been two hours since his plane touched down on the tarmac at Portland International Airport. The two secret service agents exited the plane first, followed by the President. The same exact process had taken place at least 10 times in the past two years. The limousine was driven out to the plane and four men entered it and departed immediately. There was no fanfare, there never was at his request. Josh Johnstone and Chet Linus had repeated this exercise with him on each occasion. Together they had more than 50 years with the Service. They'd had responsibility for a number of high placed officials over the years and had learned to accommodate their peculiar wishes. This man, however, had a need for privacy about him. He kept everything so close to the vest it was impossible to know what he was thinking. The fourth man knew everything, but, like his boss, he shared nothing.

They arrived at the glass monster of a condominium stuck in the middle of the Pearl District. The routine was always the same: plane to condo, condo to cigar bar; one agent inside; one out. Josh was always on the inside with Chet stationed outside in the rain. Neither ever discussed switching. It was about being familiar with the situation and the consistency over the years provided the familiarity. Jake Rappaho was the fourth man, wherever the President went, Jake followed.

They were at the same table they had occupied more than 20 times before - one from State Government; the other from the Federal Government; one openly gay, the other married for 30 years. The table was in the far corner of the room with a perfect starched table cloth in place on top of it. Everyone knew they had been linked together politically for years, each supporting the others points of view. Their appearance together was no longer a big deal to anyone.

Bruce's thoughts returned to the present and to the warmth of the hand on his left thigh. His mind was a mess, conflicts seem to cloud judgment and yet the feeling he had at this moment made the weather outside seem like an afterthought. Tomorrow was another day, another plane flight and, although Hawaii was one of his favorite destinations, this would be a trip to a portion of the Hawaiian Islands chain that he had never seen. This was not a pleasure trip in any way.

The hand moved slowly but steadily toward the rise he felt growing under his pant leg. How did it happen, how would he survive. What was the answer that he so desperately needed to know? Yet here he was in a situation that couldn't well be explained even to those he cared the most about. What would Father Patrick O'Callaghan his Catholic Parish Priest say if he knew?

The year was 2013; the 2012 election had been brutal but with the elation of the victory came the stark reality of the situation at hand. The problems were real and growing at a seemingly unstoppable rate.

As the former Senior Senator from Oregon, and now President of the United States, Bruce Gavin had watched the deficit grow and the national debt top $15 trillion. He was not even sure how many zeros a trillion had let alone $15 trillion. No question that the trillion numbers were the new billions. The President knew that one trillion dollars is simply a number that few, if any, people can comprehend, let alone your standard nine digit calculator. It has been said that a trillion dollar bills laid end to end would reach the Sun or you could spend a dollar per second for 32,000 years. He also knows that a trillion dollars can fund the military of every NATO country combined and that a trillion dollars is enough to run the Federal Government for over 100 days. Now multiply that by 15 and you get some idea of the size of the problem the President had on his hands. Something had to be done, and he had to be the one to do it.

The warmth had moved from lukewarm to hot and the urge to relieve the pent-up excitement was immediate.

# CHAPTER 1

## IN THE BEGINNING

**Sturgis, South Dakota
2010**

Sturgis Cigar Bar, the former home of Mike and Toni's used appliance warehouse, was named after the famous Motorcycle Rally held in Sturgis South Dakota. The Jackpine Gypsies Motorcycle Club started the rally in 1936. The Gypsies were founded by Pappy Hoel in 1935. It was 2010 and the 75th anniversary of the club. As motorcycle clubs go the average life cycle is three years. So to reach three quarters of a century was a major milestone.

Mike and Toni Morgan would simply not miss the event in South Dakota. At age 53 and 54, respectively, they fit the average age of the club members. In recent years the club had grown to the point that it now had over 200 members world wide.

The used appliance business was sketchy, at best. They only survived for the three years they had been at it because of the deep recession that had been going on. The recession was the primary reason George Bush left office with a black mark on the history books and Barrack Obama was inaugurated as the 44th President of the United States. Who would have thought that the United States would elect a black President in 2008.

It was the eighth rally that Mike and Toni had attended and what a celebration it was. Mike with his well worn tattoos and 300 pound body and Toni, with her very plentiful store bought boobs, fit right in. In fact, the boobs were an investment they made after attending their very first rally. If you have never been to a Sturgis event then you can't imagine why Toni would insist on a new pair that was fitting of the occasion. Needless to say, her pink leather outfit brought out eyes from every corner as they crossed the country heading for the rally on their hog. It was only when they arrived that they looked perfectly normal and fit right in. Everywhere else they looked like a side show. You guessed it, the tattoo was a Harley Davidson logo. Not bad marketing when you can get a guy to tattoo your label on his body without even asking.

"Mike, I did the bills before we took off from Portland, our business is in the tank. We had almost no used appliance sales this month. Our rent is eating us alive and at this rate we are going to go under. I'm not sure what we need to do but I've been thinking a lot about it lately."

"Really, what have you been thinking about?"

"Well, we both know that smoking has come under fire lately from all sides. People who smoke are unable to do so just about anywhere these days. The regulations have gotten stricter and now some people can't even smoke in their own apartment if the ventilation system could send the second hand smoke to others apartments."

"So what does smoking have to do with used appliances? We both smoke and have for about as long as I can remember."

"Well, I read about this club in Chicago where smoking was legal because it was posted as a smoking club and if you're going to go in you know what you're getting into."

"Toni, I still don't get what you're talking about. Would you do me a favor and dumb it down so I can understand."

"O.K big guy, here is what I think. Our warehouse is smack dab in the middle of the Pearl District. The Pearl District has taken off and is getting more and more high end. The bars and the shops are filled with men and women in their 20's and 30's. The district is no longer the dump that we have always known it to be. So I thought that with three years left on our lease that we could take our warehouse and turn it into a cigar bar. We wouldn't need to do much other than add a bar and get a liquor license. We have adequate rest rooms and the open beam ceilings will lend themselves to the atmosphere that young people are looking for."

"The cigar bar will be for smoking. Everyone would be welcome -- Men, Women, Gay or Straight. Who cares as long as they are willing to pay? I think that we can make some real money if we do this and, if so, I can stop thinking about how to sell a God damn used toaster."

"Now I get it woman, not a bad idea. What would we call it?"

"Look around, stupid; why not call it Sturgis Cigar Bar."

Bruce Gavin had known Mike and Toni from growing up on the east side of Portland. Mike was a greaser in his youth and Toni was one of those kids from the east side that could be difficult to bring home to Mom. She was attractive as hell, but the way she looked and talked presented a problem to almost every adult with whom she came into contact. The product of a broken home with a full time working Mom. Toni was on her own, did what she wanted and didn't care about anything other than Mike. Bruce played baseball with Mike in the Montavilla Little League. The park was not far from 82$^{nd}$ and Stark where his parents, Bill and Mildred Gavin, had raised him in a World War II house. The house was on Washington Street, one block off Stark. The original price was $4,000.

As a kid, Bruce did the things most other kids did. He went everywhere he had to go on his Schwinn Bicycle. He attended the same parties everyone else did. Kissed his first girlfriend with the lights out in the basement of Howard Funnel's house and did what he had to do to stay in school. His parents and grandparents were proud and his childhood was as normal as a kid's could be with a total annual family income of $4,500 and a very used 1950 Chevy. Both parents worked; his father Bill was an iron worker and his mother was a school secretary.

Mike, Bruce, and Toni would often attend the afternoon movies at the Academy Theater on Sunday afternoon. The funny thing about it was that it was always just the three of them, never a fourth.

No one in the Gavin household was religious and, thus, Sundays were spent as the second day of the weekend. He was free to roam, hang out with Mike and dream about the future. Religion was never discussed, so he had no frame of reference, or concern in anything having to do with religion.

High School was easy for Bruce. He played baseball, tried his hand at basketball and was a defensive back on the football team. Baseball and Football fit him well, his basketball days were numbered as he could barely hang on to the sixth man spot on the Junior Varsity Team. "Jump! You have to learn to Jump!" his coach would say over and over to the point that even today he hated the word. At 6 feet 2 inches he had the body to be good but there was just something about basketball that he just couldn't handle. His social life was pretty normal, however, few, if any girls, interested him. He attended all of the proms and double dated with Mike and Toni from time to time, but girls were simply not of interest at this time in his life.

The world interested him. Local politics and people's positions on issues interested him unlike everyone else his age. Most of all he liked numbers. He wasn't entirely sure why but things like budgets, income, expense all fascinated him.

Over the years the thought of going on to College crossed Bruce's mind but never interested Mike or Toni and for that matter very few of his high school friends wanted to go. It was the east side of Portland, and when you graduated from high school you went to work or went into the military.

It was during his junior year in high school that he was asked to come into the counselor's office. His grades were fair considering he really didn't care. A 3.4 grade point average was achieved with little or no effort.

Her name was Rebecca Laceful. Ms. Laceful was a well know figure around John Marshall High School. Besides serving as a counselor she was also the Vice Principal and in that capacity, made few, if any, student friends. In fact, Mike constantly referred to her as Ms. Facefull and he should know because he met with her on a frequent basis, and rarely at his request.

Ms. Laceful was not a looker. She carried a significant amount of weight and, as a result, she had few distinguishing features. Most of her features simply disappeared into her massive face and body. Even today he smiled when he thought of Mike's description of her as a watermelon with a wig.

"Mr. Gavin", the voice came out of know where. "Mr. Gavin, are you awake?" "Yes Mr. Von Burton, I'm awake."

"Would you please come up to see me after English Class, I have a message for you from Ms. Laceful."

"Yes Sir."

At 10:50 the bell rang and Bruce walked up to Mr. Von Burton's desk. "Sir, you said you have a message for me from Ms. Laceful. Do you have any idea what she would want to see me about?" "As far as I know, I have done nothing that would warrant a visit to the Vice Principal's Office?"

"No, I don't know what she wants. I was notified this morning that when you finished my class she wants to talk to you in her office. Here is the message. Good luck Bruce."

The bell rang at 10:50 AM and like the others he filed out of class but rather than go to the library to spend some time on his American History class he turned left and walked the long hallway to the administration office. The school Secretary was one of the nicest people he had met during his time at John Marshall High School. Perhaps it was due to the fact that his Mom, Mildred, was also a school secretary, but in any event, Mrs. Martin was one of the Marshall High School's staff that made his good guy list.

Mrs. Martin saw him enter the office and welcomed him with a smile and "Hello". While he wanted to say he was here to see one of the bad guys, he refrained and said, "Ms. Laceful has asked to see me, any idea what this is about?"

He thought she started to respond but the voice stopped when the door to Ms. Laceful's office opened and suddenly the entire door frame was filled to the brim with Ms. Lacful's bountiful body.

"Come in, Bruce. I have a couple of things I would like to discuss with you." He entered her office and watched as she maneuvered her huge body in such a way that she seemed to perch on her regulation-sized chair. He took the seat in front of her desk and waited for her to speak.

"I asked you to come to see me today because over the past month I have had three of your teachers come to see me about you. I should say at the outset that the subject of my conversation is positive not negative." A silent sigh of relief passed through him like a knife through butter. He was almost positive that he'd not done anything wrong enough to be called in for discipline. Still, just being summoned never failed to raise a multitude of guilty feelings – real and imagined.

"Each Teacher independently has drawn the same conclusion. They all feel you are smarter than everyone in their class and that you are so far ahead with your thinking about the subjects they are trying to teach you that you have become bored and as a result do slightly better than average work when you are capable of A+ work. The teachers who have come to see me are your Political Science Teacher, your Advanced Math Teacher and your World History Teacher."

"I looked at your grade point average and it is currently a 3.4. Not bad, but not good enough to go on to a top level university. Have you ever considered what you're going to do in a year and a half when you leave this school?"

After a moment's thought, Bruce had almost said "I'm going into the Navy" but he thought further. Finally, his response surprised even himself. "I have not given it much thought. I have great parents who care about me a lot but we are not any different than most families in my part of town. We just don't have the money to send me on to college, even a local one. But I suppose if money were not the issue, I'd consider possibly going to a local junior college."

"Well, that brings me to the second point I wanted to discuss with you. I have received notification that Catholic Charities of East Portland have received a gift from an anonymous donor that will enable them to award two scholarship grants to students at John Marshall High School in the year you are scheduled to graduate. The only catch is that if a grant is awarded, it must be to a student attending a Catholic School. Are you by chance Catholic?"

"I'm not anything." "Religion has been totally absent in my life. I have read about the religions of the world and their influence on people. In some ways I think religion could be the cause of all the wars and much of the suffering that the people of the world have experienced."

"Thoughtful answer, I'm not a very religious person myself but in this instance you may want to focus on the Catholic religion as it could possibly be the key to your future education."

"This brings me to the final point I wanted to discuss with you. Each of your teachers has expressed their belief that you have an enormous untapped potential. A potential that could take you far from the east Portland surroundings. We believe that as teachers and educators, we have an obligation to do everything we can to unleash your potential."

"So, in conclusion, I think you should consider where you are and what you want to do. If this scholarship opportunity is something that interests you, then you should look into it, study its requirements and, if desired, apply for it. I checked into West Coast Catholic Schools that would meet your academic interests and at the same time provide you with a new point of view and the opportunities that could expand your potential. The University of San Francisco fits all of the requirements. Frankly, it's too bad you don't excel in basketball because I'm told they have a great program and produced some professional players. Lastly, I would encourage you to start exploring the Marshall High School Political Science Club and consider running for class office. We all think these activities could add up on the positive side of your ledger."

"It is a lot to consider. I'm not Catholic, have never been out of the State of Oregon; don't belong to any school organizations other than the baseball and football teams. I will, however, give what you have said thought, discuss it with my folks and let you know what course I have chosen. Thanks very much Ms. Laceful. I appreciate your comments." The old girl, Bruce thought, was actually moving up on his list.

\*\*\*\*\*\*\*\*\*\*\*\*\*\*\*\*\*\*\*\*\*\*\*\*\*\*\*\*\*\*

"Toni, look at this place. Why are Greyhound Bus Depots all the same? They are old, dirty and attract a bunch of people that make us look like members of congress." "Mike, the folks you see here are for the most part homeless. My guess is they have no place else to go and like all of us they need someplace that is dry and warm."

Bruce started laughing and said, "Mike, for you to even begin to remotely look like a member of congress, you would have to loose about 200 pounds, get rid of your Harley tattoos and quit smoking. Somehow I don't think that is going to happen."

"It's almost time for the bus to leave and I've got to get back to school, but before I do, I want you to know that all of the staff and many of the students at Marshall High School are very proud of what you have accomplished in the last year and one half. We all wish you the best of luck at USF." Having said that Ms. Laceful gave him a hug, turned and headed for her car.

"Who would have thought you would get a hug from Ms. Laceful. I can tell you with all of the time I spent with that woman there was no chance I'd ever get a hug. I have a hard enough time getting one from Toni and I think she likes me."

"Don't push it big guy, if you get any bigger hugging you will be physically impossible."

"Well son, we wish you the very best, we love you and will be anxious to hear from you once your settled in. Dad and I will miss you a great deal."

Bruce had his ticket in his hand and the bus for San Francisco was departing in five minutes. Mike, Toni, Mildred, Bill and Ms. Laceful were all part of the reason he was here. It had been a whirlwind year and a half since his "come to Jesus" meeting with Ms. Laceful. He was elected Student Body President, grades improved to a 3.8 GPA, studied the Catholic Religion, converted to it and received the East Side Catholic Charities full scholarship to the University of San Francisco. The time was 4:35 PM and the date was August 2, 1974.

# CHAPTER 2

## CHINA 1950's

**China
1950's**

Woo Wong was born on October 21, 1956, on a small peasant farm just outside of Beijing, China. His birth was the result of an arranged marriage between two adults who had never met and had only minimal interest in each other once they had been introduced on their wedding eve.

Mao Tse-Tung was Chairman of the People's Republic of China, but not all was under his control. Zhou Enlai was the Nation's Prime Minister and, even though Mao claimed to lead a coalition government representing 14 separate political parties, the country was really run by the Communist Party. Officials for the Party were in charge of every level of government including the media.

The country had little industry, a valueless money system, towns with high unemployment and waves of food shortages at a time when the population was increasing by 14 million per year.

Woo Wong's parents were farmers, as well as, landlords. While not viewed as rich, they had wealth in the form of land and were in control of it. As a result, the family had been blindsided by the Agrarian Reform Law which the Party passed in 1950. Under it, the property of rural landlords was confiscated and redistributed. This fulfilled a promise by Mao to the peasants and decimated a class identified as feudal or semi feudal. Woo Wong had no knowledge of what had happened nor did he know how the action would affect him for the rest of his life.

Once the Wong's land was redistributed, the family was left with the same portion as that of a peasant. Their once plentiful number of animals and machinery were given away just like their land. The result was the parents of Woo Wong were nothing but simple peasants with little to show for a lifetime of work. At least his family had not been rounded up to account for their past. Many other landlord families had been arrested as "evil landowners". Many were charged with significant crimes and more than one million of these ex-landlords were executed between 1949 and 1951. The peasants had supported the Communist Party and they had been rewarded for doing so.

Changes also occurred in the cities. Cars, foreigners and foreign businesses all disappeared. The acceptable means of transportation became the bicycle.

Family life also changed and, herein, lies another impact on the Wong family. In 1950, Mao introduced the Marriage Reform Law which banned forced marriages. The law was very blunt: All marriages are to be based on the free consent of men and women.

Divorce was easier to get. It had been all but impossible under the old regime. Polygamy, the sale of women into prostitution, and the killing of unwanted female babies – all common practices for centuries - were banned.

The divorce occurred quickly, the Wong's applied and the divorce decree was issued. Woo Wong's father, Fin Wong, left in December of 1951 and was never heard from again. Woo was raised by his mother. He was informed much later in life that he had two sisters, both who were killed by his father, as was the custom. In order to survive and to raise her only son, Woo's Mother, Fu, found work with the State bank in central Beijing.

The government managed to control inflation by fixing wages and prices. All private banks were closed and the State Bank was established. If a company wanted to get a loan from the State Bank it had to have the support of the Communist Party.

In 1953 all private businesses were brought under state control. The owners were re-educated and forced to publicly denounce their past crimes against the Chinese people.

******************************

## Shanghai, China
## 1959


There were a 1,000 beads of sweat covering his completely bald head. His chest hair was matted and damp and his erection was already dissipated as he rolled off of her.

She was the best and the one he always asked for.

There was no romance in this affair, it was all business. Pre-paid to the Madam, including the ripped and torn lingerie thrown hastily in the corner of the darkened room. This was not a first class hotel. In fact there was nothing first class about the place.

It was the final appointment of the day. As she lay beneath his huge, fat body, her thoughts were clear. The day was over, she had been paid for her effort and now she was free to leave and return to the most important thing in her life.

Her mother, now 80 years old, cared for the baby while she was away. Just 2 years old he had no idea what his mother did for a living. All he knew was she was his mom and loved him very much.

Shanghai, China had the reputation as "The whore of the orient". Mao Zedong had led the Red Army to a decisive victory in the civil war against Guomin Dang (the Nationalist Party).

She could see the writing on the wall. Shanghai was about to lose its economic power. Mao was dead set against prostitution. What an odd position. Here was the oldest profession in the world being attacked by a man that was known to be a womanizer. He is the perfect example of "do what I say, not what I do."

It seemed so unfair. This is all she knew. Life was not easy. She had a child to clothe and feed and she could see her livelihood being taken from her. Her name was Ching Phing and her son, who was her pride and joy, was Phat Phing. She did not know why but she knew he was special and would someday grow to be a very powerful figure in China.

***********************

Being a student in China is very stressful. The weight and burden that an only child faces can be unbearable. In China education is free up until the 10$^{th}$ grade.

Both mothers knew this and while they did not know each other they shared the same values. Education was critical to their son's success and they would do everything they could to make sure it happened. They lived different lives, they lived in different towns, yet Ching Phing and Fu Wong had one thing in common. They had a male child to raise and they intended to do it in the best way possible.

The 10$^{th}$ grade was considered the first year of high school. It is also the year following the nationwide entrance for high school admittance.

Both boys understood from the time they could read and write that their schooling was critical and that in the 7$^{th}$, 8$^{th}$, or 9th grade they would take the nationwide entrance exam. Their scores on the exam decided what high school they could attend. A low score meant that the most prestigious high school would not accept them. A high score meant that you could attend the high school of your choice. The system actually operated like the University system in the United States. Students with high marks paid lower tuition, similar to someone receiving an academic scholarship to go to a US University.

Both boys scored very high and each selected the high school of their choice; one in Bejing, the other in Shanghai.

High School was not easy, it was a rigorous schedule.

They did not know each other but their schedules were exactly the same.

From 7 AM to noon they studied four classes, Chinese, Math, English and an elective of their choice. Both selected Political Science and History as their first elective.

They had a break for one hour for lunch and then returned to class from 1 PM to 5 PM.

The afternoon classes again followed the same pattern, Physics, Chemistry, Biology and an elective. Here again the boys independently selected the same thing, American History.

From 5 PM to 6 PM class resumed with either Math or English and then another elective and time to study until 8 PM. The boys were usually never home before 10 PM.

The process was repeated six days a week.

\*\*\*\*\*\*\*\*\*\*\*\*\*\*\*\*\*\*\*\*\*\*\*

In 1949 the Communist Party embarked on a series of campaigns that were designed to eradicate prostitution from mainland China.

"I'm not sure how long we have worked together Ching but it has been many years. You are my favorite girl and you have provided well for our house of prostitution. It has been a good fit and you have become the most desired of all the girls in the house. I'm afraid however that it is all coming to an end."

"I know what you mean, I have watched the Mao policies effect on our business and I think he is a total hypocrite. He wants to ban prostitution while at the same time he has nude women entertain him all of the time. I know some of the girls that have had to perform for him. What is he on now, his 5$^{th}$ wife or thereabouts? I also know as fact that he is a total womanizer."

"I have watched some of my friends be taken to the institute for re-education and I have heard their stories about what the institute is like. Sure, there are no guards but almost no one escapes. My friends tell me that they tell them at the institute that they are not fit for Chinese society."

"I'll be damned if I will be trucked off and given some sort of medical examination. The institute claims that almost all of the girls they examine have some sort of venereal disease. That is just a crock; we have never had a complaint from any of our customers as long as I can remember."

"Nevertheless Ching, it is time for you to leave the house, find a safe job and maintain a low profile until this stupid group in power goes down the drain."

"I know you are right. I will leave but I will miss the girls and you, Madam. I have enjoyed my work and the earnings I have received. As you know, I have a son to support and so I will heed your advice and leave today. Thank you for all you have done for me."

"Good Bye Ching and good luck."

Ching Phing had no mental scars and no use for Mao and his point of view. She resolved during this difficult time to insure that her son, her pride and joy, would see the other side of the political spectrum and be exposed to democracy at some point in his young life.

It was late in 1951 when her madam was arrested and taken away by Mao's soldiers. The house was closed and the girls, not rounded up, fled. She had been one who fled. With her mother and son she changed homes and began a new life working in a small laundry owned by her best friend Xu.

Laundry work was dangerous and involved long, laborious days. Usually, Ching Phing began work as early as four in the morning and she did not end her day until the latest hours of the night. A far cry from her days as a requested and pampered prostitute working in a reputable house for a woman who truly cared for her girls.

Hand laundries required many hours of manual labor. The laundry was washed in large wooden kettles of boiling water and then was strung over strong wires to dry by a coal stove. Ironing, which Ching hated, was also done by hand, using cast irons that required heating on the stove.

The three of them lived cramped together in the back of the laundry and used nothing but mats for beds. Nothing fazed her. However, her focus remained on her son and his growth and opportunity.

**************************

The term "high school" referred to the senior portion of the Chinese secondary educational process. After six years of primary education and three more years of academic study in middle school the compulsory education gave way to the senior secondary education where graduates could choose the school they would attend and the academic curriculum they wanted to pursue.

As the boys grew up and went to school in their separate towns a number of events occurred in Chinese society that would eventually shape the course of their lives.

In 1953 the national transition to communism was well underway in China. Emphasis was placed on the development of heavy industry, centralized planning, and the build up of a defense capability.

In 1954 the First National People's Congress formally elected Mao as Chairman of the People's Republic. This period in Chinese history followed the following theme " Let a hundred flowers bloom, let a hundred schools of thought content encourage intellectuals to participate in the new regime with a climate of political openness." The openness did not work and was quickly squashed by the Party.

In 1958, Mao launched the great leap forward to accelerate the development of all sectors of the economy at once. The Great Leap Forward was designed to entrench communist principles in the structure and functioning of the social system. It was characterized by the development of people's communes in the countryside and selected urban areas.

Everyone, including party members, intellectuals, professionals, technical workers and the bourgeoisie were required to work in the communes, factories, mines and on public work projects.

The Great Leap Forward did not work either. Rather than boost production it brought about food shortages, lack of raw materials, and a demoralized and exhausted population.

It is estimated that by the early 60's 14 to 20 million people died of starvation and the population shrunk.

This all combined to bring about the resignation of Mao as the People's Chairman. In a now famous quote made in 1959 Mao told the Central Committee "The chaos was on a grand scale, and I take responsibility. I am a complete outsider when it comes to economic construction and I understand nothing about industrial planning."

This statement was widely quoted and no one could be happier with the resignation than Ching Phing who knew this day would come. Her life had been most difficult due in major part to this man and she felt that it was she who was the victor and survivor and he the fallen villain.

In 1970, with both boys in high school, they watched as millions of school and university students were organized into the Red Guards to publicly criticize those in the party who were considered by Mao to be left or right of his point of view. The Red Guards received Mao's backing when he published an article endorsing their revolutionary posters and slogans, then he presided over their first mass demonstration in Tiananmen Square.

Both boys watched when the little Red Book of quotes from Chairman Mao was published. The book instilled revolutionary fervor and created havoc within the party and widespread social chaos. Mao's wife, Jiang Quing, was behind much of the havoc as she wanted to see old customs and ways of thought disappear.

The CCP and Government were crumbling and opposing political factions created their own Red Guards. Thousands died when the fractions entered into open armed conflict.

Schools, colleges and universities closed. Virtually all engineers, managers, scientists, technicians, and other professionals were criticized, demoted or sent down to the countryside to participate in manual labor. Many were jailed.

It was not until the late 1960's that the militant phase of the Cultural Revolution came to an end. The Red Guards were disbanded and many were forced to resettle in remote parts of the country.

*******************************

Fortunately for both boys by the early 70's the universities and schools were reopened as they reached university age.

Both boys excelled, selected and were accepted at the best high schools in Beijing and Shanghai available at the time. Both boys were active in their schools, both showed a strong interest in politics and history and both were focused on attending college. One in the United States, the other in China.

Both mothers were enormously proud of their boys. Both supported them financially and with all of the love you can give a child. Both were rewarded for their efforts as both boys were accepted to universities.

Fu sat quietly as she studied and listened to her son. "Mom, I have thought long and hard about my University experience. Because I have done well in school I have lots of opportunity ahead but I have decided that what I really want and need is to broaden myself outside of China. I would like to go to college in the United States. I know that it will mean that I will not be able to see you often because of the expense but I know that this is the best thing for me." "I have studied the College's and Universities on the West Coast of the United States and have found one that I think is good for me."

"What are the criteria that you have used to determine what is best my son?"

"I wanted to be in an area that has a large Chinese immigrant population, I wanted to have an institution that would provide me with a rigorous experience with small class size and top professors and I wanted an institution that had a diversity of population in both students and faculty. I also wanted an institution that has a strong political science department and one that was close to an international airport." "Last, I wanted one that provides some financial assistance to foreign students."

"It sounds like those are the right criteria. What have you decided on?"

"The University of San Francisco. It has the diverse curriculum I want. It has history as it was founded by the Jesuit Fathers in October 1855. It also is located in San Francisco which has the largest Chinese population of all of the cities on the West Coast of the United States." "I have already written to the University, sent them my records and have been advised that if I apply they will provide me with financial assistance that will pay for both my books and tuition. That means our expense would be for housing, food and airfare."

"Woo, I have worked hard to give you the opportunity to excel in what ever you choose to do. If this is something that you want, I will commit all of my resources to see that it will happen. You must make the decision, but I will support you in any way I can."

Phat Phing selected Shanghai Jiao Tong University. The year was 1975 he was 18 years old. The University was well known to him and had a history going back to 1896 when Nanyang Public School was founded in Shanghai by an Imperial edict issued by Emperor Guangxu.

At the end of the Chinese Civil War in 1952 the new Communist government adopted a policy of creating soviet-style specialized schools. Under this policy, some faculties of the university were incorporated into other universities. At the same time, engineering faculties from outside were absorbed to create a specialized engineering university. In 1956, the government decided to send a significant amount of its Faculty to Xian to help create another top engineering school. Once completed, the school was officially renamed Shanghai Jiao Tong University.

The University was located in Xuhui District of Shanghai, formerly a largely Catholic area. The buildings on campus were influenced by American architecture, while the main gate, which was built in 1935, is of traditional Chinese style.

Phat Phing had focused on this institution since childhood and the smile on his mother's face when he was accepted could not be adequately described.

# CHAPTER 3

## FATHER PATRICK O'CALLAGHAN

**San Francisco, CA**
**1967**

Father Patrick O'Callaghan grew up in the Mission District of San Francisco. He was born in the City, and attended Saint Philip's grade school, Sacred Heart High School and the University of San Francisco. You couldn't be more Catholic than Father Patrick O'Callaghan.

He experienced all that the city and the church had to offer. He was an alter boy and was a kid who liked to hang around with the teachers and priests who were most assiduously involved in the church.

As one might imagine he was also exposed to the other side of the Catholic Church. As a boy, he was exposed to the dark side of the Catholic Priesthood. He was in the fifth grade.

The first incident occurred on a Thursday afternoon at his local church. It was a school day but as often was the case he stopped by the Church on his way home to hang around with whoever was present. This day Father O'Riley was working in his office on a sermon he was to give the following Sunday.

Patrick stuck his head in the office and said "Hey Father what's up". Father O'Riley, looked up from his study, saw young Patrick and invited him in. "Thanks for stopping by Patrick. I need a break and your being here provides that opportunity.

Come on in and close the door." Patrick did not realize that once the door closes it automatically locks.

"Patrick, you have been spending a lot of time hanging out here at the Church. Do you have any interest in learning more about what it means to be a priest and to giving yourself to the Catholic Church?"

"I have thought a lot about the Church and what it means to me. It seems that each year I become more interested in it and in the teachings. I don't know much about it but I think it might be a career that I would like to learn more about."

"Well Patrick, I can tell you from experience that becoming a Catholic Priest is not easy and it takes a significant amount of study and will power. The Church is always in need of people who care deeply about others and believe in the principles of Catholicism."

"Father, what has it been like for you?"

"Well, my son, it has been a series of learning events spread over a lifetime of study, prayer, and thought. I learned from a very early age that this is what I wanted to do and what I wanted to be. My life was shaped by the Priests I learned from. It is they who helped me to grow, understand feelings, and also to understand my own body."

"What do you mean by that Father?"

"Well, as you know, one of the principles of becoming a Priest is to commit yourself to Christ and to the teachings of God and the Church. One of those principles is the principle of celibacy. Celibacy is a very interesting and sometimes difficult concept to embrace because it is counter to many of the physical things we experience as we grow up."

"I'm not sure I understand?"

"Well, as you grow and mature like you have begun to, you pass through puberty and your thoughts can begin to influence your body. For example, many young men get physically excited when they see young women who are partially clothed. Some are temped by these feelings and eventually succumb to them by making love to the woman or, to be technical, they have intercourse with them. Obviously, if this happens you are no longer celibate and have disregarded one of the principles of Priesthood. Let me tell you a story, Patrick, about my own experience."

"When I was about your age, I had a Priest that I liked very much. I had spent hours with him and was sure that I wanted to be like him in every way. To that end he was the one that helped me decide that the Church would be my life."

"One of the things he talked to me about early on was celibacy. Our conversation was much like the one we are having today. In the course of that discussion, he explained to me that just because you are a Priest does not exempt you from the feelings that suddenly come from within your body. He told me you need to be aware of the feelings, understand them and learn to deal with them."

"To help me understand this, one day he opened his robe when we were alone. To my surprise he had nothing on under it but he was having the feelings that he had talked to me about. He wanted me to see what happens when you have them and what you can do about it. He asked me if I had ever seen an erect penis before."

"I told him that I had not. He also asked me if I had ever touched one. I obviously had not but was fascinated with what I was looking at. My priest then went on to talk to me about the pleasures of masturbation both individually and with the help of another man. He explained that it provided the relief needed to remain celibate. He said that it would help me to avoid the temptation of a woman and would help me to maintain my celibacy vow to the Church."

"Father, did you touch it?"

"Yes I did and I never forgot it. He helped me to learn to masturbate and the ways one man can help another. It was a wonderful life lesson."

"Wow, Father, that must have been something to see."

"Yes, Patrick, would you like to see what it looks like?" Patrick nodded. With that, Father O'Riley opened his frock and stood before Patrick with a total erection. "Patrick, you must learn to touch it and to deal with the excitement that comes with it. You may touch it now if you would like."

\*\*\*\*\*\*\*\*\*\*\*\*\*\*\*\*\*\*\*\*\*\*\*\*\*\*\*\*\*

## Washington, D.C.
## 2013

A parish needs two things under common law to become a parish. First, it needs a body of Catholics within a fixed boundary and, second, it needs a named priest with responsibility for the parish. Parish boundaries vary in different parts of the world. Catholics can generally choose to worship in any church that they find convenient or appealing.

A parish is the center of the spiritual life of most Catholics. It is there that they receive the sacraments. The parish priest is the clergyman in charge of the congregation.

A busy schedule is typical of all Catholic Parishes. The seven sacraments are the center of parish life. Traditionally there is Mass daily and on Sundays according to the pastoral needs. There are offered confessions, as well as, other forms of prayer and an assortment of social events.

Father Patrick O'Callaghan was the Parish Priest for St. Peter's on Capitol Hill.

St Peter's Parish was founded to serve the growing population of the eastern part of the city as well as the Capitol and the Naval Yard. It was established in 1880 and was the second Catholic Parish established in the City of Washington.

The parish also has a school for children. It is an active parish, conscious of its place in the historic district close to the Capitol, the House office buildings and the Library of Congress.

Of significant importance is that this is the parish of the President of the United States and his wife.

\*\*\*\*\*\*\*\*\*\*\*\*\*\*\*\*\*\*\*\*\*\*\*\*\*\*\*\*\*

## San Francisco, CA
## 1967

His young hand reached out and touched it. It was hard and the tip was wet. He looked at Father O'Riley and smiled. Father O'Riley looked back and smiled. "Remember, Patrick, experiencing this is between you, me and God and it is never to be shared with anyone else.

He removed Patrick's small hand and proceeded to show him how this most magic of male organs worked. The strokes came fast and furious, while there was no sound, the ejaculation both surprised and fascinated Patrick. It was also a moment when he knew that his would be a life with God and with other men. There would be no need for women in his life and his life would be devoted to the Church.

********************

## San Francisco, CA
## 1974

Throughout his grade and high school years Patrick spent more time at the Church than he did anywhere else. He continued to learn from Father O'Riley and was now able to assist him in relieving the pressure associated with celibacy and in turn Father O'Riley was able to assist him. Each year the enjoyment became more.

He began college at the University of San Francisco and selected his major as Religious Studies.

His road to becoming a priest was not easily traveled. He had studied the requirements extensively during high school. He knew that following college he would need to be accepted as a candidate for the seminary. He needed not only academic ability but physical, mental and spiritual health. He felt that the volume of effort he had given his church during his youth would demonstrate his earnest commitment.

He knew that the priesthood was not just for saints and that the ability to regularly seek forgiveness from God was an asset in his vocational aspiration.

While he was still exploring his own sexuality, he knew that religious orders and dioceses seek people who have a strong sense of their own emotional needs. Candidates to religious life must have the gift and talents to live a life of celibacy. Some said that living a life of celibacy requires abstinence from all sex but Father O'Riley had taught him differently, and thus, some sexual behavior between he and a non female partner was simply a means of releasing the pressure.

The more he learned the more he understood that to be a potential candidate for priesthood one must have a capacity and a willingness to love and serve God as a celibate priest. There has to be an openness to learn and grow mentally and intellectually. One must also be blessed with the desire and willingness to embrace the challenge of the twenty-first century with joy, hope, and enthusiasm.

As he entered USF, Patrick was sure he had picked the right profession and had the background and dedication to it that would take him far within the Church.

The late 60's and early 70's were the days of sexual revolution in San Francisco. Gay and Straight exploded with open sex for all to see. The Haight and Castro districts of the city fostered the movement but it wasn't just confined to these well know parts of San Francisco. Sex clubs and bath houses popped up all over the city.

Gay men have been meeting for sex in bathhouses since the late 1800's throughout the United States. In California, as in other states, all homosexual acts were illegal and considered as crimes against nature well into the 20th century. As a result, men who were caught engaging in sexual acts with each other were subject to arrest and public humiliation.

This, however, went by the wayside in the 1960s and throughout the 1970s. The bathhouses evolved from being discreet places that were talked about in hushed tones to the modern, fully licensed establishments, that operated to serve the needs and wants of the gay community.

In San Francisco, if you were into heavy duty bondage and real rough sex you got a room at the Slot on Folsom Street. If that place was booked up for the night you could find accommodations at another bathhouse, the Handball Express.

In the late 1970s, statistics showed that the average club customer was white, between 30 and 35, earned about $12,000 per year and stayed at a club for approximately five hours during which he climaxed three times.

In San Francisco, State Representative Willie Brown's Consenting Adult Sex Bill passed in January 1976. As a result, gay bathhouses and the sex that took place in them became legal for the first time in California

Several bathhouses featured weekly movie nights where Hollywood films were shown, especially gay cult classics, such as, "Some Like it Hot" and "The Women".

One of the factors which made the holidays more festive for gay men was the fact that many bathhouses threw parties for their patrons on holidays such as Gay Pride Day, Thanksgiving, Christmas and New Year's Eve. These parties were a great service to gay men whose families had rejected them and for who the holidays represented a gloomy time of the year.

Patrick was surrounded by all of this as he entered his freshman year at USF. It would be his college years that helped him define his own sexuality.

The date was August 2, 1974. Patrick's parents along with Father O'Riley were packed in the family station wagon with all of the things that one would select as important to a teenager. They were headed up Highway 101 toward their final destination, the University of San Francisco.

# CHAPTER 4

## HAWAII

**Beijing, China**
**1974**

It was August 1, 1974. Fu Wong stood in the main terminal at Beijing International Airport. Her pride and joy, Woo, was about to board China Airlines flight 59 from Beijing to San Francisco.

"Well, Mom, now that the time is finally here I am feeling nervous. Not about my decision to go to USF but about the plane flight. Last night I thought about the fact that I have never been out of China nor have I ever been on a plane."

"I also thought about us. I realized that in my entire life I have never been away from you. All of this time I never worried about anything because you were always there and I now realize you did all of the worrying for both of us."

"Woo, you have nothing to worry about. People fly all over the world. I'm told it is one of the safest means of travel. Certainly it is safer than trying to negotiate traffic in downtown Beijing."

"As for my worries, you have solved most. You have earned a full scholarship to USF which pays for most of the expense. We can afford the air travel but we will have to be wise about how many trips you make back and forth. You are fully ready to accept the challenge and the uncertainty that awaits you. There is no mother on earth that is prouder of her son than I am at this moment. Like you, I am well aware that this is the first time in 19 years I will be away from my baby." "We will get through this and we will both be better for it. You will see."

The loud speaker echoed in the main terminal at Beijing International Airport. China Airlines flight 59 from Beijing to San Francisco was boarding.

"Now boarding passengers on flight 59 to San Francisco, rows 22 to 40." He looked at his ticket it was 27A.

He looked at his Mom for one last time. His adam's apple jumped and he couldn't stop the tears as they poured from his eyes. He held his mother close and told her that he loved her and could never express the appreciation for her sacrifice on his behalf.

She looked at him for what would be the last time for an unknown period. Her words for him were simple and clear. "Woo, be the best you can be." She was confident that he was special and that this experience would only be one more step on the road to his ultimate success.

Woo turned and entered the boarding gate, handed the ticket that said seat 27A on it to the airline attendant and proceeded to board his 13 hour flight to San Francisco.

He was too excited to sleep. Most of the regular passengers who travelled regularly ate a brief meal, had a couple of cocktails, then pulled a blanket over themselves and began a six hour sleep. Woo just looked out the window as though he was in a coma. His thoughts wandered all over the place. He thought about his Mom, USF and San Francisco. His mind jumped from one thing to another until everything became a blur.

It seemed like just an hour had passed since the plane taxied down the runway, lifted off and headed directly east. The fear and excitement he experienced had not yet left him.

The announcement brought him back to reality. The Captain's voice was loud and clear. "We are starting our decent to the Hawaiian Islands. We expect to be on the ground in Honolulu, Hawaii in approximately 30 minutes. Please place your seats in the upright position and fold your tray tables up.

Our stewardesses will be moving throughout the cabin to assist with any last minute preparations."

Woo was very familiar with the Hawaiian Islands. He had studied them for years and found them to be one of the most interesting places on earth.

The islands were an archipelago of eight major islands, several atolls, numerous smaller islets and undersea seamounts. They are located in the North Pacific Ocean and extend some 1,500 miles from the island of Hawaii in the south to the northernmost Kure Atoll. The islands form the U.S. State of Hawaii. Once the plane touched down, Woo knew he would be entering the United States of America.

Maui was the Valley Island but it carried a fascination for Woo that he could not explain. He had studied the whaling operations conducted from the port of Lahaina since he was a child. He admired the long white sand beaches and more than once told himself that he would have a place here and experience it with his Mom while she was still able to enjoy it. In fact, that thought became a focused goal for much of Woo's life.

From his studies Woo also knew that the islands have many earthquakes, generally caused by volcanic activity. They were also subject to tsunamis, great waves that strike the shore. Tsunamis are most often caused by earthquakes somewhere in the Pacific. The waves produced by earthquakes can travel as fast as 400 to 500 miles per hour.

The climate of Hawaii is tropical but it experiences many different climates depending on altitude and weather. The islands receive most rainfall from the trade winds on their north and east sides also know as the windward side. The coastal areas in general and, especially, the south and west flanks or leeward sides tend to be drier. Woo knew this to be true and that was another reason he liked Maui and its whaling town, Lahania.

The voice of the pilot made it clear that they were now on final approach to the city of Honolulu. There would also be a rest stop during refueling and the passengers would be allowed to leave the aircraft for a period of two hours before reboarding for the final leg to San Francisco.

Woo could not wait to leave the aircraft and set foot on the United States of America. This would be the next step in his long-held dream.

The airport was large but did not match the size of Beijing International. It was, however, very well decorated. It contained lots of food concessions that carried American food like hot dogs and hamburgers.

Woo had only read about hot dogs and hamburgers. He had never tasted or even seen one. Here at the airport you could order a hot dog with everything on it for 25 cents. The hot dog would be Woo's first purchase in the United States. He loved it and savored every bite.

As he wandered around the airport he came across a display on the military significance of the Hawaiian Islands. He remembered that this was the center of the Japanese attack on the United States during World War II but did not think too much about the Island's strategic military advantage. The subject interested him, however, and he spent the next two hours reading and studying the exhibit.

Pearl Harbor, as it is now known, is mentioned in the accounts of early Pacific Voyages as Wai-Momi or Water of the Pearl.

The earliest explorers and traders who wrote accounts of their visit to the Sandwich Islands seemed to give most of their attention to Hawaii, Maui and Kauai, but in 1789 Captain Nathaniel Portlocks mentioned Pearl Harbor in his writings of his visit on the British vessels King George and Queen Charlotte.

Woo read the history with great interest, it was not until the late 1800's that Pearl Harbor became a factor in the military defense of the islands. The Harbor appeared to afford the best and most spacious harbor in the Pacific.

Woo read that in 1873 the USS California, with Rear Admiral A.M. Pennock brought to the islands a military commission consisting of Major General J.M. Schofield and Brevet

Brigadier General B.S. Alexander. This commission proceeded under secret instructions from the Secretary of War, William W. Belknap to examine the different ports of the Hawaiian Islands with reference to their defensive capabilities and their commercial facilities.

In Major General Schofield's report he wrote the following, "Its shores are suitable for building proper establishment such as magazines for ammunition, provisions, coal, spars, rigging, etc., while the island of Oahu upon which is situated could furnish fresh provisions, meats, fruits and vegetables in large quantities.

It was in January of 1887, the United States Senate in secret session modified the convention providing for the extension of the original reciprocity treaty of 1875 to include the following "His Majesty the King of the Hawaiian Islands, grants to the Government of the United States the exclusive right to enter the harbor of Pearl River, in the Island of Oahu, and to establish and maintain there a coaling and repair station for the use of vessels of the United States and to that end the U.S. may improve the entrance to said harbor and do all things useful to the purpose aforesaid." The treaty was ratified by the Hawaiian Senate and signed by the King on October 29, 1887.

Woo read the definition of a Treaty. He had read the word many times but did not fully understand its meaning. The display noted that a treaty is a binding agreement under international law. Treaties can have many names like international agreements, protocols, covenants, convent exchange of letters, however, all of these meant the same regardless of what the treaty is called. They can be loosely compared to contracts. The central principle of treaty law is the maxim "pacta sunt servanda" "pacts must be respected".

It was very clear to Woo reading this history that the military significance of the islands was clear to the United States almost 100 years before and that vision would only be expanded in the years ahead.

On February 2, 1900, the first official Naval Station in Hawaii was established in Honolulu. Over the next 35 years the Navy expanded and improved the facility. In the early years the station grew slowly and not always at an even pace.

With World War I, the demands to establish Pearl Harbor as a first class naval base capable of taking care of the entire fleet in case of war, precluded its usefulness as a commercial harbor.

By 1934 over $42,000,000 had been spent on the development of Pearl Harbor. Within the confines of the Naval Yard, were now located Minecraft, the Fleet Air Base and the Submarine Base. By 1940, appropriations for the improvement of the naval establishment had exceeded $100,000,000.

Woo read that with the huge amount of money invested in Pearl Harbor came the growth in naval personnel. The harbor housed 586 enlisted men in 1925 and more than 1000 by 1936. It was very clear that the advanced base at Pearl Harbor was a critical strategic military advantage in a main defense triangle.

Woo finished his hot dog which made a huge impression on him. He wasn't sure why he was so fascinated with the exhibit before him but he wanted to finish reading it before he had to reboard his flight in less than an hour. The question was should he or should he not get another hot dog. He decided against it. Too much of a good thing can be bad his mother use to say.

He had come to the last segment of the exhibit and had a half hour to go before boarding. This section of the exhibit he knew the most about so he was able to move through it quickly. It focused on the Japanese attack on Pearl Harbor.

Operation Z was a surprise military strike conducted by the Imperial Japanese Navy against the United States Navy Base at Pearl Harbor, Hawaii on the morning of December 7, 1941.

The attack was intended as a preventive action in order to keep the U.S. Pacific Fleet from influencing the war that the Empire of Japan was planning in Southeast Asia, against Britain and the Netherlands as well as the US in the Philippines. The base was attacked by Japanese aircraft in two waves with a total of 353 planes launched from six aircraft carriers.

It was this attack that caused the United States of America to enter into World War II.

Four US Navy battleships were sunk and four others were severely damaged. The Japanese also sank or damaged three cruisers, three destroyers and an anti-aircraft training ship. One mine sweeper was also lost. In total, 188 US aircraft were destroyed, 2,402 personnel were killed and 1,282 were wounded.

The end result was well documented. The United States and its allies went on to defeat the Imperial Japanese Army and Navy.

Nevertheless, the war was enormously costly to the United States, and as the display indicated, solidified the Hawaiian Islands as one of the most strategic possessions when it comes to power in the central pacific and far east.

This was not lost on Woo as he again showed his boarding pass and found his way to Seat 27A.

His flight left on time and the five hours remaining to San Francisco seemed to pass very quickly. He even found himself dozing off from time to time.

# CHAPTER 5

## THE CONVERGENCE

**San Francisco, CA**
**1974**

It was August 3, 1974. The bus from Portland, Oregon, arrived at the San Francisco, California, Greyhound bus depot at 11 AM. The depot was located at 425 Mission Street in downtown San Francisco. It was not located in a great area but Bruce knew from his own experience in Portland that that was the case almost anywhere you went. The terminal was busy even at 11 AM but it was clear by just looking around that it served far more people than bus patrons. It also served as home for a number of folks that simply had nowhere else to live. The restrooms made that even more evident.

He looked around. He was tired and alone for the first time in a city that, by his standards, was huge. The bus ride had been long and he had not slept much as everything he saw was something new. He was tired from his bus ride, but excited about his next step, which involved getting to the campus of the University of San Francisco, completing registration for his first semester of college and meeting his new, pre-determined dorm roommates.

*******************************

The drive up from the Peninsula took no more than one hour from his parent's home to the campus of the University of

San Francisco. John O'Callaghan, his wife Patricia, and their son Patrick were joined on the trip by Father Michael O'Riley. Father O'Riley had become a treasured friend of the family and both John and Patricia looked up to him as a mentor to their son Patrick. His faith in Patrick and his influence on Patrick's dedication to the Catholic Church were very apparent to John and Patricia and, as a result, it was only fitting that he should join them for this next major step in Patrick's life. Little did they know that Father O'Riley's influence was significantly greater on Patrick in ways that they simply could not imagine. In fact, it was only one week ago that Father O'Riley had entered Patrick for the agreed upon last time. It was time for him to move on with his life and, both, while they enjoyed the experience, knew and agreed it had to end. It was 1:30 in the afternoon of August 3rd when they arrived at the school's administration building.

*******************************

Flight 59 from Beijing, China to San Francisco, California touched town on the tarmac at San Francisco International Airport at noon on August 3rd 1974.

Woo Wong watched as the plane made its final approach over the waters of San Francisco Bay. It was a crystal clear day with no fog. He had expected fog as he had read that the coldest place on earth was a summer in San Francisco.

The city of San Francisco glimmered in the distance up ahead. Woo was well aware that the city in the foreground housed approximately three quarter of a million people. The average age of the population was 36 and almost equally split between men and women. He knew about the Chinatown district off of Grant Street and the many aspects of his culture that were still practiced by the Chinese in San Francisco.

Woo also knew that USF, his ultimate destination, was situated just off Golden Gate Park and not that far from the Haight-Ashbury district of the city. The phenomenon known as Flower Power was still going strong and like so many other aspects of San Francisco life he had read about, he was eager to experience it.

The wheels touched down and he had finally arrived. The thrill he felt was almost impossible to contain.

Woo Wong cleared customs with no problem, picked up his three bags at baggage claim and walked out of the International terminal to the cab stand.

He knew his final destination was 1600 Holloway Avenue in the city. He handed the cab driver the directions he had been given.

Woo had never been on a real freeway before. He could not believe the 280 freeway, it was as beautiful as a highway could possibly be. No advertisements, no garbage, no clutter. What an impression this new city was making on him.

He arrived at the admissions office at 2:30 PM.

******************************

All of them arrived at the admissions office at a different time on August 3rd. Each had been accepted and each had applied for housing on campus.

The admissions process went smoothly for each of them. USF had its act together and it was apparent to each of the students. The school was prepared, organized and passed on the needed information to each of the boys. Once the admission process was completed each of the boys was provided with their housing information.

All of them had been assigned to the same triplex dorm room. The triplex dorms at USF were old but very functional. Each triplex had three separate bedrooms, a joint living room, 2 bathrooms and a small kitchen. The dorm room assigned to the three boys was T-31 in Complex A.

In addition, each boy was assigned to attend the new student orientation. Fall Orientation began on August 10th. It was a two day session that was mandatory for undergraduate students. There was a separate international student orientation that was also required.

Families were allowed to attend but, in the case of the three boys, none of them would have family available.

Bruce Gavin was the first to arrive at the triplex dorm. He

was followed in the early afternoon by Patrick O'Callaghan and last to arrive was Woo Wong.

Bruce selected a bedroom and threw his stuff on the bed. He had brought two suitcases which held just about all of the clothes he owned. He then headed out to explore the campus.

Not long after Bruce had left, Patrick O'Callaghan arrived with his parents and Father O'Riley. There was one room with suitcases in it but the other two were free. Patrick selected one of them and with the help of his family unpacked his bags and arranged his stuff in his closet. Each room had a desk and study lamp besides a chair, bed and bed stand. Father O'Riley helped set up the desk while Patrick's mother folded and put away his clothes. Once that was completed everyone knew it was time to leave. Hugs all around, a special kiss from his mom and then they were gone. Patrick just sat on his bed studying his room where he would live for the foreseeable future.

As he was about to get up and go out to see the campus, the door opened and in walked Woo Wong.

"Hi, my name is Patrick O'Callaghan."

"I am Woo Wong from Beijing, China. I am very glad to meet you Patrick."

"We have a third roommate but I don't know who he is. His bags are in the bedroom on the right. I threw mine in the center bedroom but you can have the center or the room on the left, it doesn't matter to me, Woo".

"No problem, I will just take the one that is left. "

"Do you have anyone with you or did you travel to USF by yourself?"

"I am alone. This was my first plane flight and my first trip out of China. I am both tired and energized at the same time."

"Here, let me help you with your bags, I see you have three with you."

"Yes, my mother packed them, so I'm sure they will be very neat and organized. She is much more organized than I am. Two of my bags have my clothes and the other has the stuff for my study area."

"Woo, you speak perfect English, how did you learn it so well?"

"In China we study multiple languages. I have taken English since I began school. I also speak French."

"What do you say we unpack and then take off together and check this place out? I know the campus pretty well so I can be your tour guide."

Once he had unpacked and organized his things, he and Patrick set out to see the USF campus.

USF's main campus is located on a 55 acre setting between the Golden Gate Bridge and Golden Gate Park. USF's nickname is "The Hilltop." Woo had no idea that the Jesuit-Catholic identity is rooted in the symbolic vision of St. Ignatius of Loyola, the founder of the Jesuit order. Jesuits are characterized by a dedication to both the life of the mind and the encounter with the world. For this reason, the campus offered distinguished intellectual and humanitarian majors notably in the fields of higher education, human rights and social justice.

Woo was, of course, attracted to the campus for non-religious reasons. Nonetheless, his nature was aligned to the Jesuit call to justice as evidenced by their work in community service, and reflection retreats both on campus and abroad.

The campus had approximately 8,000 students from 75 countries, all 50 states and is ranked in the top 15 universities nationally. The University holds the renowned Center for the Pacific Rim.

"Woo, this is the University Center. Let's stop for a Coke and get something to eat. The University Center is where students hang out between classes or when they want to get together informally. The book store is attached to it so it is handy."

"When I was on the flight across the Pacific, we had a brief stop over in Honolulu and I had my first hot dog. It was really good, do you think they have them here?"

"Yep, we can order them along with our Cokes. Let's order and then sit at the table by the window."

Once they had their orders they grabbed the table by the window.

"Woo, how in the heck did you get to USF from Beijing, China?"

"Well, I wanted to study at the University level in the United States. I researched the Universities on the West Coast and USF had everything I wanted. I wanted to be near an international airport, I wanted to be in an area with a large Chinese population and I wanted a school with small class sizes, great professors and a strong political science program. USF had all those. It also didn't hurt when I applied for a scholarship that I got one. Everything just fit into place." "What about you Patrick?"

"Well, I am from the peninsula which is just south of San Francisco, about 40 minutes by car. I am very interested in studying religion and am considering becoming a Catholic Priest. As you probably know, USF was founded by the Jesuits in the mid 1800's. The school has a very strong religion program which just fit with me. I did not want to be far from home so it was an easy choice for me."

While Patrick and Woo were exploring on a surface, not substance basis, Gavin was housed in the Richard A. Gleeson library located in the center of the lower campus. The library holds more than 680,000 books, 130,000 journals, 2,200 periodical subscriptions and 900,000 other materials including government documents. The library was also where the Political Science Club was located and that was what brought Gavin to the place.

The political "bug" had bit him in his last year and a half at Marshall High School. He wanted to have the experience carry over into his time at USF and he saw no better way than the Political Science Club. He didn't know where it would lead him but his goal was to be Student Body President of the University someday.

Patrick and Woo headed back to their dorm room. They opened the door and were greeted by a guy that was much bigger than either of them. "Hi, my name is Bruce Gavin, I'm from Portland, Oregon."

"Hi Bruce, nice to meet you, my name is Patrick O'Callaghan and this is our third roommate, Woo Wong."

"Hi Bruce, it is a pleasure to meet you."

"I hope you guys didn't mind, when I arrived I just threw my bags in the first room there on the right. They are all pretty much the same but if either of you would like to trade, its fine with me."

"No problem, we had the discussion earlier and we all are happy with the rooms we have. We have been out exploring the campus. I'm from around here so I was able to show Woo some of the buildings."

"I was out on campus as well. I wanted to see the Political Science Club and learn how to join it. I am interested in Political Science and the school is well known for its program."

"Interesting, I am from Beijing, China and am also interested in Political Science, in fact it is one of the reasons I picked USF."

The boys hit it off instantly and the conversation was flowing between them at about 100 miles per hour. Suddenly one of them looked at his watch and said "Its 7:30, are either of you hungry?" The others realized that they were starving and had not eaten much since well before Noon. Woo and Gavin had no idea where to go to get food, but Patrick was familiar with the city and had a suggestion.

"It is our first night together. Our first dinner together should be something we will always remember. I have a suggestion. I think we should grab the Geary Bus and take it to Van Ness then walk up to Tommy's Joynt." Woo and Gavin didn't have a clue, but, were starving so the plan was hatched and the boys headed for the bus stop.

Tommy's Joynt, located on Van Ness Avenue in San Francisco, has been owned and operated by the Harris, Veprin and Pollack triumvirate since 1947. Tommy's Joynt is one of the older restaurants in San Francisco and, therefore, shares a great deal of history with the City.

It is an original hof-brau and has become one of San Francisco's longest living institutions. It is located in the crossroads of the City at Van Ness and Geary. "Welcome Stranger" decals itself above the front door. The restaurant promises hot food and cold drinks at an affordable price. The restaurant proclaims that the atmosphere is like the food, no frills.

Patrick explained that the Joynt could best be described as a hungry man's Mecca. He said, "If you want lettuce on your sandwich, better go to some fast food shop because Tommy's Joynt wants you to taste the meat they carve.

Woo had no idea what Patrick was talking about but he was all for the experience. The meal was great; the conversation better.

Gavin ordered the corned beef, Patrick the stewed lamb and Woo the short ribs and beef meatballs. The house special was buffalo chili which Patrick ordered to be shared by the group.

Their conversation lasted until three in the morning. At 4:30 AM, Woo woke up with the stomach ache of his life. Go figure, he was not ready for hot dogs and American Buffalo chili.

# CHAPTER 6

## SALEM

**Salem, OR**
**2010**

It was 6:30 PM. Bruce Gavin sat in his office at the State Capital located in Salem, Oregon. It was overcast and there was a slight drizzle. He looked out and saw so many government workers heading for home with no umbrellas. Oregon was an interesting place, it rained or was overcast and drizzled for nine months of the year but no one used an umbrella. They all had hoods or stocking caps and that was all that was needed. In Washington, D.C., the umbrellas came out as soon as the summer thunderstorms occurred. He thought how he hated the D.C. weather and thought back to his time in east Portland where neither he nor his family ever used an umbrella.

He was the Senior Senator from Oregon. He had spent the last two days in conversation with his wife Dorothy about the most significant decision of his life. He knew that tomorrow he must board a flight back to Washington and give them a decision. Dorothy was all for it. 100% behind it. He was far from sure and needed this last opportunity to think.

He met Dorothy in law school at Stanford. Dorothy was an heiress. The family was originally from Nebraska which is where Dorothy grew up. She was an only child and was spoiled rotten from the day she was born. Nevertheless, Dorothy was smart and physically about as attractive a woman as he had ever met.

At 6'2" and 185 pounds, Bruce had managed to maintain a physical presence that still turned a few 40 something's heads. Dorothy was blessed with a perfect body and face. She was 5'8", weighed 125 pounds and had a body that she openly told friends measured 35-24-35. Each summer, for as long as she could remember, guys would spend hours around her with the slim hope that they might get a brief glance of her breasts. She was well aware of this, and in order to insure few went home disappointed, she purposely wore low cut tops which provided just enough of a view to keep them coming back for more. She was in total control; had been then and was today.

Their romance was a whirlwind. It began in their second year of law school and was soon consummated under a large pine tree at Stanford University. Dorothy was not one who could take a house and make it a home. With the exception of clothes, she had no taste in color, design or anything that had to do with interior decoration. Perhaps the talent was there hidden someplace, but as long as he had known her it had never surfaced. She always had others who could fill in the gaps that were only apparent to those who knew her well.

What Dorothy was good at was sex. Since the day he met her she "oozed" sex. She knew that God had given her a magnificent base model which she had enhanced along the way. The ultimate body was designed to do one thing and that she did over and over. She knew how to do it, how often to do it, when to do it and where to do it. She also never got tired of it. Most guys would have died and gone to heaven if they had Dorothy to themselves.

In the early days, Bruce was into it and able to keep up the pace she demanded. He never forgot the first time she had made love to him. It was on the campus of Stanford University about 8:00 PM one evening. It was summer, the sun was about to go down on their picnic. It had been great food and wine. She was "dressed to kill" in the smallest shorts one could possibly get on and a loose fitting top with no bra. She had jumped on the flower power bandwagon and with tits like hers the movement allowed her to acceptably show others what she had. She was the aggressor. Before he knew it, she had removed his shirt and hers as well. She sat on top of him straddling him with her long legs. She looked down into his eyes and mouthed the words, "I want you now". He just let it happen. His shorts were off before he knew it. He had no idea how she got hers off but she did and he knew he had nothing to do with it. She had left her black g-string panties on more to tease him than for anything else. She knew it would just add additional sexiness to a situation that simply didn't need more. This is how she approached making love. The panties were simply another piece in the puzzle. It was part of the puzzle and served its purpose. It, however, didn't take much time for that piece of the puzzle to come off. She moved in such a way that she never left the top of him. She had him where she wanted him and she had him in her before he knew it. She controlled the process. It was over in less than 10 minutes with the two of them climaxing at exactly the same time. When it was over he felt a wonderful sense of one with her. Little did he know that that would be the first of three exact repeats over the next two hours.

He remembered waking up the next morning, almost unable to walk. To say he was sore was an understatement. He never asked her how she felt the next day and she never brought it up.

The last 10 years had been different. Their interests had seemed to slowly grow apart when it came to sex. He was sure that it was not her but rather him. He simply wasn't interested and was pre-occupied with other things. He was pretty sure that she had not lost interest in that activity and he was sure she had figured out a way to satisfy her needs without him.

He was admitted to Stanford after a great undergraduate program at The University of San Francisco. At USF he was both Valedictorian and Student Body President. Stanford University Law was the only school to which he had applied, and he was accepted on early admission. He and Dorothy were the same age. Both graduated in law and both with a significant interest in politics. She went on to clerk for a Federal Judge in Salem and he entered the world of politics. They were married not long after graduation.

The wedding was held in Chicago and was beyond anything he could have imagined. He remembered the occasion not as one of joy but almost embarrassment for his family. The east side of Portland was a long way from downtown Chicago and for a family that still lived in the $4,000 World War II house he grew up in, it was a total mismatch. He wasn't even sure how his folks were able to afford the flight back to Chicago. Thankfully, Dorothy's family paid for everything with no questions asked. The wedding itself let him know that he was entering a truly new world.

Bruce was very proud of his father. At the rehearsal dinner his father stood and addressed the group. He was a man of few words. He said, "We are very proud of our son as I'm sure you are of your daughter. Their achievements are remarkable and each is capable of climbing mountains on their own. Based on their past achievements, we know that they will reach the top of any mountain they try to climb. Our hope for them is that with their combined love they are better together than they are alone. We wish both Bruce and Dorothy the best that life can give. We have little to give but our love, but we want you to be assured that we will give all of it."

With that he walked over hugged Bruce and kissed Dorothy on the cheek.

The wedding the next day was almost royal. No expense had been spared. The bride was spectacular and even that superlative seemed short of the mark. Her father was never so proud when he walked her down the aisle thinking that he only wished her mother could be here to see this. As she walked down the aisle she looked ahead at the people standing. On her side of the aisle was Brit Tiffany, her maid of honor. Brit was her best friend and her roommate at Bryn Mar. On Bruce's side of the aisle stood his best man, Jake Rappaho. At 6'7", Jake was the tallest person in the room. Sitting in the second row, on Bruce's side of the aisle, were two special friends, Patrick O'Callaghan and Woo Wong. Patrick had come from Washington D.C. where he was very involved in his studies for the Priesthood at Dominican House of Studies. Woo Wong had flown from China and would not miss this occasion.

Their bond was with politics and, in her case, power. She loved being the wife of the Senior Senator from Oregon and made no secret of the fact that to be the First Lady of the United States would be a dream come true. Many times he was certain that they were simply not a good fit. He was a kid from the east side of Portland. She was rich beyond anyone's measure. She was both elegant and arrogant. She was not a social climber. She had been born on the top of the mountain and it was everyone else who was climbing toward her. Together they had grown apart. They had little in common other than politics, but somehow they had stayed together with each of them gradually living their separate lives. Each with there own secrets.

Bruce ran first for Mayor of Eugene, Oregon, then on to the State Senate. That was followed by a very successful role as the Governor of Oregon and then on to the Senate of the United States. Each election was challenging but he won each by a landslide. He sat here in his office tonight as the Senior Senator from Oregon.

They lived in a mansion on the Willamette River just outside of Portland in a place called Charbonneau, a private neighborhood within the city limits of Wilsonville in Clackamas County. It was named for Jean Baptiste Charbonneau who was the son of Sacagawea. The place was special to Bruce. He was very involved in Oregon land use. Charbonneau was one of the oldest planned communities in Oregon. Its construction helped lead to the adoption of land use planning in Oregon and set the urban growth boundary in an effort to attempt to prevent urban sprawl. Bruce had led the legislative fight for this land use concept and that had served as the foundation for their selection of Charbonneau as a place to live. It also was conveniently positioned just off Interstate 5 about half way between Portland and Salem. Portland was his favorite town but Salem was where he had his State Office in the Capitol.

Sacagawea was a Shoshone Indian who traveled with the Lewis and Clark Expedition from 1804 to 1806. She was the slave wife of the expedition's French Canadian guide, Touissaint Charbonneau. Sacagawea was the only woman in the party and she carried with her, her son, Jean Baptiste. Her actual death is debatable but it is generally assumed that she died in 1812. After her death, it is known that William Clark adopted Jean Baptiste and Sacagawea's daughter as well.

He was fascinated with Oregon history and could have day dreamed about it for hours. But that was not what was on his mind this evening.

Barack Obama had been in office for two years. During that time he had faced one major crisis after another. To his credit he had been able to move health reform forward, if that is what you called it, and at the same time put some Band-Aids on the Country's financial crisis. It didn't change the fact that there were growing structural imbalances and high levels of debt among G8 nations, both of which were unsustainable. Like a fault line gathering pressure underground, these trends represented a growing systemic risk under the global financial markets. It was not difficult to see that these economies would be unable to outgrow their problems. The burdens of debt, higher taxes and more regulation would at best act as a "ball and chain" on economic growth. He believed that they were headed into a deflationary spiral in asset prices and in confidence, not just in the United States, but world wide.

The only bright spot seemed to be Asia. He had shared his concerns and discussed the financial crisis with his college friend, Woo Wong, on many occasions. Both agreed that the world was on the brink. The United States National Debt which now exceeded $13 trillion was a root cause of the problem. If something is not done to reduce it, it would ultimately lead to the end of the United States as he had known it. The thought was overwhelming. The collapse of the US Monetary System would create world havoc and the United States would, without a doubt, lose its position as a world power. Something needed to be done and he strongly believed Barack Obama was incapable of doing it. It would take the 45<sup>th</sup> President of the United States to deal with it and, at that moment, he knew it would be up to him. He had his answer and would be prepared to tell them at the end of his plane flight tomorrow.

# CHAPTER 7

## RED YELLOW GREEN

**San Francisco, CA**
**1976**

The China Airlines Jet was in line on the runway at San Francisco International Airport. It was third up. In front of it were two US airplanes. A United flight bound for Chicago and an American Flight headed for Denver. The China Airlines flight was due to head directly west to Beijing, China. There would be one stop in route, Honolulu, Hawaii.

The thought of a hot dog crossed his mind and he smiled.

It had been two years since he left Beijing on his first airline flight. He had not forgotten the look on his mother's face that day. He kept in regular contact with her mostly by mail due to the expense of long distance calls. He had completed his second year at USF and was going home for the summer. What a whirlwind the last two years had been. There had been so much to see and do.

His roommates had been great, but after two years with each other, they had agreed it was time to split. Woo wanted a place of his own. He wasn't sure if Bruce and Patrick would live separately or move in together. San Francisco had been so new to all of them but after two years in the heart of the city, they all knew it well and were very comfortable on their own.

The friendship they had made would last forever as would the memories.

Bruce and Woo followed a similar path at USF. Both were political science majors with an eye towards law school following graduation. Both were active in the school's political organizations and both were involved in student government. Woo was now the President Elect of the International Students Association and Bruce had run successfully for school office and would be the incoming Student Body Vice President when he commenced his fall semester in September.

Patrick followed a different path. He majored in religious studies which provided him a broader view of the religions of the world. He was a devout Catholic and was President of the Catholic Student Association which was a "big deal" at the Jesuit School. Patrick's goal was to pursue a religious career and enter the seminary after graduation.

The hippie subculture was still going strong in the early 1970's and the Haight was at its heart and about a stone's throw from the campus of USF. Woo loved to watch people and understand trends in society. He was fascinated by the fact that the hippy culture had a major effect on so many things. Among them, fashions, values, food, music, sex, movies, and so much more. It was happening before his eyes and it was so different than the culture he had grown up with.

Sexual Freedom, a tolerance for Gays, and a free form lifestyle were all part of San Francisco in the 1970s. The bath house revolution, live rock concerts and drug experimentation were all for the taking in the city. Proximity to Golden Gate Park meant that the students at USF were in the heart of it all, and most students experienced part, if not all, of it. This was certainly true of Bruce, Woo and Patrick.

Woo thought back to some memorable events. There had been many firsts in his life in his first two years in America.

He remembered his first rock concert at the Winterland Ballroom in San Francisco. The concert featured the Grateful Dead. It began early in the afternoon and went until after midnight. Their improvised music was best appreciated at live concerts, and their shows generally had a positive, happy atmosphere, as the band and the audience interacted with each other to create a special environment. The air smelled of pot, which was everywhere. The girls were free and the spirit was open. It wasn't a question of would you sleep with someone after the concert, it was a question of who or how many.

Woo, Bruce and Patrick went to the concert together. Woo did not know what happened to Bruce and Patrick after the concert. Each went their separate ways. Woo didn't have a clue what the others were up to but he did know what he did. He scored for the first time in his life and thought that Bruce and Patrick must have as well. Neither Bruce nor Patrick ever brought up what happened that evening, nor did Woo.

When the sun rose the next day Woo found himself sleeping on his blanket alone in Golden Gate Park. She was gone. He never forgot that night. He never learned her name, but didn't care. This, he thought, was San Francisco at its best.

He remembered his first visit to a bathhouse with Bruce and Patrick. While there were women present, the vast majority of people were guys and, from what he could tell, most of them gay. He saw stuff that he didn't think was possible and he didn't feel comfortable the moment they entered. He told Bruce and Patrick so. He never visited a bathhouse again. The scene turned him off completely.

He was sure that Bruce had gone to them on more than one occasion. Woo sensed that the bathhouse scene for Bruce was such that he could take it or leave it. It just was a diversion from the norm and, thus, only of passing interest.

Patrick, on the other hand, seemed to love the bathhouses. He openly let the guys know when he was going to one. He said they were relaxing and took his thoughts away from school and his studies. This amazed Woo because Patrick was so religious. It just didn't seem to make sense. Needless to say, Woo applied one of the things he had learned in America. "It just is not my problem, nor do I care, so what happens is fine with me."

One of Woo's most memorable firsts was his visit to San Francisco's Chinatown.

To Woo, Chinatown was the epicenter of the city's history. The town was not quite 100 years old but it had a presence about it that bridged the history of San Francisco. After the 1906 earthquake, Chinatown had been completely rebuilt. It was an incongruous mix of Edwardian structure with applied Chinese detail. The original neighborhood was established in 1848 before the Gold Rush. The first Chinese immigrated to San Francisco when a woman and two men arrived on the sailing ship, Eagle. It was the same year Sam Brannon announced the discovery of gold at Sutter's Mill, California.

In July of 1853, Old St Mary's Cathedral, the first cathedral in California and the tallest building in town, was built on the corner of Grant and California Streets. The Church was right in the heart of Chinatown. It only seemed appropriate that the church's granite foundation was quarried and cut in China.

Chinatown had so much Woo could relate to. Chinese lore dictated that evil travels in a straight line, so the side streets of Chinatown were a labyrinth. When one walked these streets, the smell of incense almost always led to Taoist shrines and temples. The city's oldest Buddhist praying place was located in Chinatown. There were many produce markets where fruits and vegetables, bok choy, spring onions, mushrooms and slender purple eggplants were in abundance. There were herbalist shops where herbs and animal parts strange to westerners' tastes but inextricably tied to the culture Woo had gown up with.

The place was special and in the last two years Woo had spent many hours exploring, teaching Bruce and Patrick about it, and reminiscing about the home he had left so long ago.

While Woo was so excited to see his Mom and his friends in Beijing there was a second purpose to his visit. He had agreed, as incoming President of the International Students Union at USF, to speak at Shanghai Jiao Tong University in Shanghai. Woo had been contacted by Phat Phing who was President of the Chinese Student Cultural Center at Jiao Tong. Phat Phing had a method to his madness.

Phing was interested in learning about exchange opportunities in the US. He had completed his second year at Jiao Tong and his research had focused on USF. He was interested in the experience for all of the same reasons Woo had decided to attend.

Phat did not know Woo but he learned that Woo was from Beijing and was attending USF on a full scholarship. He also learned that Woo was President of the International Students Union. As such, Phat thought "he could kill two birds with one stone." He invited Woo to attend a student conference at Jiao Tong and to share his experiences in the United States at the University of San Francisco. The students would gain the experience of his knowledge and he would know if he should pursue the exchange opportunity.

And then there was Ming Tai.

Woo had met her through the International Students Association. The purpose of the Association was to help new students from foreign countries adjust to the University and to the city they were about to be immersed in.

Ming was the daughter of a Chinatown merchant. She was beautiful, his age, and about to enter her junior year at USF. She was also an American Citizen born and raised in San Francisco.

Their relationship evolved over their second year at USF. Eventually, it was consummated in one of the most beautiful moments he had ever experienced. Since that night they had been almost inseparable. They both knew that the relationship was for now, for the moment. They knew at graduation Woo would return to China where he would begin his career in politics. Neither wanted to discuss the future. It was just too hard to think about. Ming's family loved him. He was made to feel a part of everything the family did but they too knew that Ming was an American Citizen and would not leave her family to join Woo in China. It was complicated and sad. Both Woo and Ming did their best to never think about it.

The engines began to roar and the McDonnell Douglas DC 10 headed down the runway, lifted off, and headed west toward Hawaii.

The anticipation of his return was almost too much for Fu Wong. In a matter of hours, her only son would arrive at Beijing International Airport having completed his first two years at a foreign university. So much had happened since his departure that she was sure they would be up half the night talking about his experience and what was going on in China.

Since his departure the tension between the radical and moderate factions of the Chinese government continued to rise until September of 1971 when Lin Biao staged an abortive coup d'état against Mao. Lin Baio was killed in a plane crash as he attempted to flee the country. His death marked the beginning of the end for radicals and the ascension of the moderates. Fu was sure that Woo would be pleased with the news. It was also during 1971 that the CCP government received international recognition when it assumed the China seat at the United Nations replacing the government in Taiwan.

By 1972, Mao had developed a suspicion of the Soviets and this was further questioned by the moderates to such an extent that it was reflected in a shift in China's foreign policies. Rapprochement with the United States was confirmed when President Richard M. Nixon visited China in February of 1972. By 1973, the moderate's policies of modernization were formally adopted by the CCP and at the First Plenum of the 10th National Party Congress, held in August of 1973; Mao made his last official appearance.

1973 also marked the rehabilitation of Deng Xiaoping, who was reinstated as Vice Premier.

The DC 10 touched down on runway number 3 at exactly 11:00 AM. Fu Wong was there and this time with tears in her eyes.

# CHAPTER 8

## GEORGETOWN

**Portland, OR**
**2010**

"Bruce, what time is the driver picking us up?"

"He should be here at 8:00 AM sharp, so you will have to put something on besides that new bra and panty set you have been checking out in the mirror all morning."

"What you don't like it?"

"Needless to say, you can wear clothes. It doesn't much matter what you put on, or how little there is of it, you still have what it takes, kid."

"I'll take that as a compliment, dear, I might say they are pretty rare these days. Have you thought any more about our discussion of the last two days?"

"Not much, I think we both agree we need to do this, not just for the country but for ourselves. I am ready to take him on and based on what you have told me, I think you're ready to be the First Lady."

"Yep, no question about that."

Dorothy slipped a dark brown suit over the bra and panty set and transformed herself from Victoria Secret Model to a serious business women.

"Do you know where Petite Crêpe is?"

"Nope, I don't have much patience for that piece of crap

and actually, if the truth were known, I hope he jumped into the Willamette River."

"Here Petite, come to momma baby."

The limo arrived right on time. "You know, if we pull this thing off we will not be back to Oregon except for limited periods of time for the next four years. I will miss it. Looking at the falls at Oregon City this morning, they are really something. I was reading the other day that the falls are the largest waterfall in the Pacific Northwest and the 18th largest in the world by water volume."

Dorothy just looked out the window as the car headed up 205. She didn't say anything nor was she interested in what Bruce was talking about. Her thoughts were entirely on how best to become the First Lady.

"You know, Dorothy, when I was a kid I spent a lot of time on that hill over there. It is called Rocky Butte. I would ride my bike over there and shovel horse shit at Reds Riding Academy. It took me three years but, eventually, I was a guide and to me it was a big deal. There used to be a prison on the Butte in those days. It was the Multnomah County Jail. Some of my best memories were spent at Reds."

Bruce was talking to himself. Dorothy was off in another world.

The Senior Senator from Oregon did not check in as others did at the Airport. The driver passed the main terminal and took a security entrance that allowed the Gavins to access the Boeing 767 directly. It was a public flight and would soon be filled with other passengers but the Gavins would be onboard in their first class seats before the public began to enter. The state of Oregon had developed this procedure for the security and convenience of its senior public servants.

The flight would take about five hours and a driver would be waiting at Washington National to take them directly to the scheduled meeting.

Both were now in agreement that they had made the right decision and were in this for the long run. Both wanted this very badly - He for the people of the United States; she for herself.

It was almost 5:00 PM when they arrived in Washington. The driver met the plane. The Gavins were the first to disembark. The driver greeted the Senator and his wife and put the bags in the car and then headed directly for the Republican Party Central Headquarters. Michael Iron, the current Chair, was waiting for them and for the decision that all had hoped for.

They arrived to a warm welcome. All went directly to the main conference room and the door was closed. Mr. Iron asked the Senior Senator from Oregon if he had made a decision on the matter at hand.

The Senior Senator from Oregon looked directly at him and said:

"Mr. Iron, I firmly believe that Barack Obama's Presidency has been a disaster. He is either unwilling or incapable of doing his job. The economy is in shambles, the government is failing and Americans are losing hope. The national debt is at $13 trillion with no end in sight. I think it is now clear that Barack Obama was not ready to be President and all those who supported him, many of whom are my friends, feel that they have been let down."

"I believe that we can turn this mess around and I am willing to accept the party's support to try to do it. Mrs. Gavin and I have discussed this in detail and what it will mean to us both personally and professionally. We are ready to accept the challenge and would be very appreciative if the Party was to support us in our efforts. We have a great deal to do before 2012 but we believe that if we start now we can lead this country out of this mess beginning in January of 2013."

Everyone in the room stood and clapped. Both Bruce and Dorothy thanked everyone and shook hands or hugged everyone in the room. Bruce was into the handshakes and Dorothy into the hugs. The majority of the folks in the room were men and they loved Dorothy's hugs.

Michael Iron told both of them that he personally and all of the members of the Republican Party were in total support of their decision and that the party was unified in supporting him in his candidacy for the office of the President of the United

States. There would be no Primary to select the Republican to run against Barack Obama. All the time and effort of the Republican Party would be spent supporting him. There would be no dilution of funds. Never before in modern day presidential politics, had there been such unified support. Advertising agents and political consultants all across the country would view this as a black day.

The driver had waited and was ready to take them to their home in Georgetown. Nothing was said when they entered the car. Both were tired but also energized. Both knew that it would not be easy but it would be a very interesting next two years.

Their house, located on M Street, with a view of the Potomac, was perhaps the best home in Georgetown. Bruce could not relate to it but lived there out of courtesy to his wife. This was Dorothy's house. She picked it, she had the designers design it, and she staffed it. It was designed to make a major impression on both visitors and those attending the constant parties she planned.

They arrived home about 9:00 PM.

They were exhausted and knew that beginning tomorrow they would be on the front page of every newspaper and television station in the United States. They showered, she put on a black lingerie set and they made love for the first time in three months. It was great for her, so-so for him.

Sleep came easy for both.

As they expected, the Headline in the Washington Post the next morning was SENIOR SENATOR FROM OREGON TO CHALLENGE OBAMA IN 2012. The article went on to say that Republicans were united in their support of him. Republican Party Chairman Michael Iron was quoted as saying "all of the party's resources will be used to retake the White House. President Obama will be a one term President. We are united in our support of Senator Gavin."

The New York Times carried the story on the front page. The headline read: WATCH OUT - SENATOR GAVIN PLANS ATTACK ON OBAMA.

The Los Angles Times headline read: NEIGHBOR FROM NORTH TO TAKE ON OBAMA.

And the Portland Oregonian carried the headline: LOCAL BOY MAKES GOOD –WATCH OUT OBAMA.

The first strategy meeting was scheduled for Tuesday at 10:00 AM at the Republican National Headquarters.

Bruce was not surprised when he entered the conference room at exactly 10:00 AM. Sitting at the large table were a group of 20 people. He knew them all. Some had been with him for years; others he knew from prior campaigns. Michael Iron had done his homework and assembled the entire group with a simple call to each that said "He has accepted the challenge and will need your help. Our first meeting will be tomorrow at 10:00 AM here at the office. Please change your schedule and be present."

Dorothy was by his side as they entered. She was still glowing from the morning news and the thoughts of being the First Lady of the United States of America. This had been a goal of hers for years. She always got what she wanted, and this should be no different.

The most important person in the room was Greta Hunter. Greta Hunter had been the Campaign Manager for Bruce Gavin in every election he had participated in since graduation from law school. She had never lost an election and to him she was absolutely irreplaceable.

Greta was an attorney and a classmate of Gavin's at Stanford. She was 5'1" but her size did not reflect her superwoman will, drive and initiative. She was not a physically attractive person and had never married. Her job was her life and her life was her job.

Sitting to the right of Greta Hunter was Jake Rappaho. Jake was an American Indian who grew up on the Warms Spring Indian Reservation at Mapuin Oregon. Jake was tall, large, and muscled. Jake and Bruce went to college at USF together. Jake attended on a full athletic scholarship in basketball. Somewhere along the way the Oregon connection between the two stuck and they became great friends during the last two years Bruce attended USF.

Jake's nick name was "Hatchet". The name was given to him by Bruce almost 25 years ago and it had stuck. Jake could cut through anything. Any time there was a hurdle to jump, a bad story or rumor to be squashed or a battle to be fought, Jake was at the forefront of the issue. He was aggressive, and a formidable competitor at every task undertaken. Most people simply learned not to cross him. Those few who tried suffered the consequences. When needed he also doubled as a body guard for Bruce.

He loved working with Greta, had served as her Assistant Campaign Manager frequently in the past, and the respect the two had for each other was clear to everyone.

Jake was totally loyal to Bruce in every respect. He knew Bruce inside out. He knew the secrets Bruce kept to himself. He also knew how to keep the secrets safe from those would use them against Bruce. Jake knew more about Bruce than anyone including Dorothy who actually knew very little about the man she married.

Sitting next to Jake was Sally Overman. Sally was the Communication Chairman and would handle all items related to the media and press releases. She was a Communication Major at University of Southern California and had worked extensively as a copy editor, writer and beat reporter at the LA Times following graduation. After five years she went back to school at UCLA and received her master's degree in Journalism. A veteran of multiple campaigns with Bruce, she was well qualified for the task at hand and had the total support of her boss.

Next to Sally was Mac Foster. "Little Mac", as he was known, was barely five feet tall but he headed the Policy staff, one of the most important positions the campaign would have. Little Mac was the smartest guy in the room. He knew it and Bruce did as well. There wasn't a policy issue that Little Mac didn't understand. He could dissect a policy from the left, the right, and the center and he knew what it took to have the American public agree with the positions that Bruce took. Little Mac got his undergraduate degree in public policy at Harvard, then went on to MIT for his masters and doctorate degrees.

Lilly Langoon sat next to Little Mac. Lilly had the least amount of education of the entire group but she was street smart. She understood the working class, related to their needs and had proved over the course of multiple campaigns that she was able to squeeze money from a rock. Lilly would direct the fund raising strategy. Lilly reminded everyone of Erin Brockovich. Erin Brockovich was the unemployed single mother who brought an entire community together and almost single-handedly brought down Pacific Gas and Electric. Her line "It's the tits, Bob" will live on forever in the minds of those who must rally folks on major issues. She used everything she had and it worked. Lilly had the same skill.

Sitting next to Lilly was Gretchen March. Gretchen was the technology wizard who grew up in California's Silicon Valley. Everything Lilly needed to accomplish had to be tied together with technology. Gretchen was the former Vice Chairman of eBay. She was smart and rich. She loved working with Lilly and together they were a team that few could reckon with.

John Swift was the legal brain in the room and would head up both compliance and legal. He had worked with Bruce on many legal issues in the past and was extremely well versed in the law. John was still actively serving as the Dean of the Law School at Georgetown University.

The job of scheduling and advance would fall to Pete Bailey. Pete was Gretchen's significant other. They had worked together on Bruce's behalf on several occasions. He was the most organized of the entire crew. Everything fit into a puzzle and Pete knew where the pieces were and how they best fit together.

These eight key players were the Department Directors. The others in the room worked for each of the eight. They had all been hand-picked and they had all worked previously for Bruce and were loyal beyond any question.

Greta opened the meeting. "Thanks for coming, while I

think you all know each other I want to go around the table and make the introductions. All of you here have a major role to play in the upcoming campaign so it is important that everyone understand everyone's role."

"We have developed a national political strategy that will focus on making progress in all 50 states. To some extent we are talking a page out of Obama's book. He used a similar strategy to beat John McCain."

"Our goal will be to appeal to the broad base of the American Public. I want to try and win each and every state, even if the margin is narrow."

"We have one theme for this campaign. We will focus on the economy of the United States and the current national debt. Normal Americans can't live by writing checks that bounce because they have no money in the bank; neither can the United States Government."

"We also will bring significant attention to the national debt and its impact not only on the United States but on the World. We plan to hammer that message home at ever opportunity."

"I know that the 50 state strategy will be the most ambitious strategy that we have ever attempted. It is only possible because the Republican Party has said there will be no primaries, the entire party is backing Senator Gavin."

"We will have access to all of the resources of the Republican Party which will help because a 50 state campaign will be expensive. I want you to know that only one President has won every state and that was in 1820 when James Monroe ran unopposed and carried all 23 states."

# CHAPTER 9

## SHANGHAI JIAO TONG UNIVERSITY

**Beijing, China**
**1976**

The McDonnell Douglas DC 10 arrived exactly on time at 11:00 AM at Beijing International Airport. Fu Wong stood with tears in her eyes as he walked through customs and into her arms. The stoic look she had on her face as he departed two years ago was gone. She could not stop the tears of joy.

"Mom, I can't tell you how much I have missed you" he said as he held her tight in the middle of the International Airport.

"It has been too long and I have much to tell you." "Woo, I told myself that I would not cry on this occasion but I can't help it. I have arranged for a taxi to take us home. My new apartment is not far from the State Bank and thus I can easily walk."

"Mom isn't the taxi expensive."

"Yes, but you are worth it. The bus will take too long and I want to start spending time together sooner not later."

"Mom, I bought a slide projector that I have brought home. The reason for it is I have over 1000 slides to show you of my stay at USF. I think that a picture will be worth a 1000 words."

"I have organized the slides by month from the day I arrived until now. They paint for you a picture of what I have seen and what I have done."

"Great Woo, that sounds like a wonderful way to spend the rest of the day."

Once home and on the couch they began, Woo discussed each slide in detail before he went on to the next.

At shortly after midnight, Woo looked at his Mom and said, "I think I'm exhausted. Time for bed, we can continue with the slide show tomorrow."

The next morning over breakfast they talked about Chinese politics. "Mom, I'm aware of the fact that the moderates have started to gain popularity. What has happened to Mao?"

"He has not made a public appearance since 1973. The moderates are now led by Deng Xiaoping who is Vice Premier. The radicals and the moderates are constantly at each other. I think that Jiang Quing, Mao's wife, is at the center of the conflict. I don't like her, but I keep my feelings to myself." "Woo, have you heard of the gang of four?"

"No."

"Well, Jiiang Quing had three principle associates that were known as the Gang of Four. The group wanted to oust Deng. They launched a media campaign against Deng."

"What were their names Mom?"

"Zhang Chunquao, Yao Wenyuan and Wang Hongwen." "The group once had power but I think most look at them today as a counter revolutionary force and most blame them for the worst excesses of the societal chaos that has plagued our country for the past 10 years."

"I'm not sure what will happen but I feel in my bones that something is going to. You should follow these developments. I think they will someday serve as a political learning lesson."

"Mom, do you know anything about Shanghai Jiao Tong University?"

"No, I obviously know of it but that is about it. I have been told that it ranks very high as a Chinese University."

"I have learned that the University is changing as we speak. Since the adoption of the reforms Shanghai Jiao Tong University has increased its vigor and vitality. I am told that there is a strong emphasis on National Security and that many of the courses now being taught are designed to build leaders that will protect and grow China." "I wrote to you about my first stop in Hawaii on my way to USF and about the exhibit that focused on Hawaii and it's history. It has a lot of military significance and I'm told that the courses taught at Jiao Tong focus on this as a subject matter."

"What kind of courses would that be Woo?"

"Well, Naval architecture and ocean engineering, along with systems engineering and optical fiber technology."

"You have always expressed an interest in the world's oceans, Woo, so I understand why this University might be interesting to you." "It sounds like meeting Phat Phing, seeing the University and giving your talk will be of great interest."

They were well into their third day of 35 millimeter slides when one appeared of a Chinese girl. She was sitting on a park bench in Golden Gate Park which was just south of the USF Campus. She was smiling and looked very happy. She was small but very pretty and dressed in a traditional Chinese outfit.

Woo said nothing but Fu could see that this was a special picture and person to her son. Finally Woo said this is a picture of Ming Tai.

He explained that Ming Tai was a Chinese American. Her parents had immigrated to the United States in 1953. They were not fans of Mao Tse-Tung or China's transition to socialism. With emphasis on the development of heavy industry, centralized planning and the build-up of defense capability it was clear to Ming's family that China was following the Soviet Union and they wanted no part of it.

Ming was born in Chinatown and was an American Citizen. He explained that he had met her through the International Students Association and that she had become one of the most important people in his life.

Through her eyes and guidance, he had been able to see the American side of China. San Francisco was home to the largest community of Chinese outside of China.

Woo explained to his mom that the first Chinese immigrants had arrived in San Francisco in 1848 and the district had many significant dates associated with it. Among them Woo mentioned the following:

1.  Earthquake and Fire, Chinatown destroyed
2.  Chinese Chamber of Commerce formed – Chinatown rebuit
3.  Chinatown Public Library opened
4.  Chinese Exclusion Act Repealed by Congress and grants Chinese aliens naturalization
5.  Chinese Historical Society of America was founded
6.  Miss Teen Chinatown Pageant was established and Ming was crowned queen in 1968

Woo explained that since its establishment San Francisco's Chinatown had been a highly important and influential part of the ethnic Chinese immigrants introduction to the United States. He was proud to tell her that Chinatown is by no means a chintzy, tourist trap.

He went on to tell Fu that Ming was the only child of Wang Tai and his wife Chang. Wang was a successful merchant in Chinatown and imported goods for sale to both visitors and local residents. He ran a very successful business and hoped that his daughter would some day take it over.

Fu was most interested in the excitement in her son's voice but with the threat of putting a damper on the conversation she said "Woo, if you continue to enjoy this woman and fall in love with her, what would you then do with the rest of your life?"

Woo knew this was coming and said, "Mom, this is a subject that I have thought endless hours about. I am Chinese and will always be. While I enjoy America and the things it has to offer, I could never live there. This is an important relationship for me but it is for the moment. It cannot last for a lifetime. I plan to return to China following my graduation in two years."

They left the subject at that and ended the conversation.

He left Beijing at 11:21 at night and arrived in Shanghai at 10:00 AM the next morning. His train trip was pre-paid by the International Student Association at the University.

He was greeted at the train station by Phat Phing, who introduced himself as the President of the International Students

Association. Phat told him that he would also serve as his host while at the University and that he would stay with Phat in his dormitory on the campus for the night.

Phat was larger than Woo by about 6 inches in height and about 50 pounds in weight. Phat was clearly an athlete who worked out on a regular basis and it showed in his physical condition.

Woo spent the day as a tourist. He was fascinated to learn about the campus and its long history. Over lunch he learned more about Phat and was surprised when Phat openly described his family situation, his mom and her life, and the debt he felt to her for her love and kindness all of these years. Woo could not believe the similarities.

When the subject turned to politics and study, here again the two boys were in lock step. Phat was very interested in politics, public policy and the defense of the country. He was studying political science but had decided to major in oceanography and military defense.

He told Woo that he was most interested in learning what life was like at the University of San Francisco and that he himself was considering spending a semester abroad in the coming year.

The two hit it off in every way and the evening went much later than they thought. At dinner they were joined by other students and the conversations and drinks went well into the night.

Woo slept very soundly. The next morning he was scheduled to give his talk at Chi Wah Center. Phat had told him he had no idea who or how many might show up. He said he was optimistic that they would have a good turnout because, with the fall of Mao and the movement toward liberalization, there were many students interested in learning about democracies.

Woo and Phat arrived at the Center 10 minutes before Phat was to make his opening remarks and introduction. To their amazement the Center, which holds 573 was jam packed and there were students waiting outside in line who would be unable to see his presentation. To accommodate them, the

Center had set up speakers outside for the students who were unable to get in.

Woo had never been before a group of this size in his life but he was not at all intimidated by the number. He knew the message that he would deliver and he hoped that it would be received positively.

Woo had thought long and hard how he would approach his topic. He decided that he would give them only one side of the equation. He would not try to compare China to the United States, nor would he compare the Chinese Education System to the United States Education System. He would just give them the United States side of the equation and let them make the comparisons on their own.

He wanted to cover the following subjects in his prepared remarks and then take questions:

- Overview the United States as a country. He would talk about its size, about the states including Alaska and Hawaii and how the government works in Washington, DC.
- The culture, the diversity and the people and how they differ across the states.
- The education system at the University level and the subjects available to students.
- Promote USF and, to do so, he wanted to talk about the University and its educational focus. This was where he would give them his view of the educational and life experience of a foreign student in the United States Educational System.
- Talk about life in the present. It was the 70's, the flower generation had taken hold. Music, lifestyles and food were all undergoing change.
- Lastly, he wanted to talk about democracy and how it was viewed by the people of the United States.

Woo began his prepared remarks by saying "it was almost two years ago today that I ate my first hot dog."

# CHAPTER 10

## 2010

**San Francisco, CA**
**2010**

It was six thirty in the morning. Greta Hunter sat patiently in the lobby of the Fairmont Hotel at the top of California Street in San Francisco.

She was waiting for the boys to show up. They were normally late. She was always on time. She glanced at the headline in the San Francisco Chronicle. The headline read: "UNCONSTITUTIONAL" SAME SEX MARRIAGE BACKERS REJOICE AS FEDERAL JUDGE STRIKES DOWN CALIFORNIA'S PROPOSITION 8.

About time she thought.

She looked around the lobby of the old hotel. It had opened in 1907 after a one year delay due to the earthquake of 1906. For over 100 years the hotel has stood as the venue of choice for glittering balls and presidential visits.

He wasn't President yet but she knew he would be in a couple of years and she was sure they would return to this hotel like so many Presidents had in the past. She also knew she would be with him, not as his Campaign Manager like she was today but, as his Chief of Staff.

The fund raiser last night had gone well. In one night, and thanks in great measure to Howard Kland, they had raised

$1,750,000. Not bad for a Republican in the heart of Democratic Country.

Howard Kland had come through for him before on a number of occasions. He was the President of Kland Enterprises. Bruce was never sure if Howard had more money than Dorothy's family but he knew that they definitely played in the same sandbox. Both his family and Dorothy's were listed as two of the top 100 richest families in the world.

Bruce had met Howard through baseball beginning in Little League and then in high school. Howard had gone to Grant high school right off 39th Avenue on the east side of Portland, Oregon. Needless to say it was a much nicer area than the one Bruce, Mike and Toni grew up in. Bruce and Howard played for different Little League, high school and Babe Ruth Leagues but they had been brought together as teammates on the East Portland All Star Team every year as long as they could remember.

Howard did his undergraduate and graduate school work at Stanford. Bruce was at USF so they managed to stay in touch through college. When Bruce selected Stanford Law School they were back together again. Howard was a businessman. He was only interested in making money and he was good at it. His first investment was in a bike pedal that your shoe fit in. He made his first million by the time he started high school.

Howard was not a politician but he understood the importance of politics and, generally, agreed with the policies Bruce had advanced over the years. Howard was the one person that Greta had called in advance of the fund raiser to brief him on the campaign's major strategies. She wanted to make sure that the positions they were about to take would not be too radical and turn off the likes of Howard and his friends. She was pleased when he reassured her that he could support each position outlined.

When Bruce returned to Oregon after school at Stanford to begin his political career, Howard stayed in California and eventually settled in a Pacific Heights mansion that overlooked the Golden Gate Bridge and Treasure Island.

Bruce was not sure of all of the ventures Howard was involved with but he knew that oil and gas played an important role.

Hosting the fundraiser for Bruce was easy. Howard just made a few calls, hosted a wonderful dinner, and the campaign put almost another $2 million in the pot.

The boys arrived in the lobby at 20 minutes to 7:00. They were 10 minutes late, but not bad by their standards.

They headed up to the Venetian Room for breakfast. This was the most elegant room in the hotel. It was on top of the hotel and had a complete view of the city. It was not normally open for breakfast but when the Senior Senator from Oregon wanted a quiet place to talk it was always made available.

Jake Rappaho was at his side as usual. It had been that way as long as Greta could remember. His size and appearance made him stand out. In fact Greta had thought on more than one occasion that he could have been the model for the Indian seen outside of so many cigar stores.

Greta had the floor at breakfast and both men listened to her intently.

She began by saying that she and Little Mac had identified eight major issues that the campaign would focus on. Little Mac had developed a policy statement on each issue and this morning she would summarize each for both of them. She also noted that the campaign would veer from the traditional Republican positions in order to appeal to a broader base of the American public. She noted that Little Mac basically ignored the religious right in his strategy and also ignored those Republican "hawks" that always wanted to fight something or someone. Both groups simply got in the way of winning, and winning is what this was about.

Greta began by listing the eight.

1. The economy, national debt and its impact on the future of the United States
2. The war in Afghanistan
3. Immigration

4. Equal Rights to include Gays in the Military and Gay Marriage
5. China
6. Out of control government entitlement spending
7. Wall Street
8. World Disarmament and the elimination of all nuclear weapons

Greta paused and looked at both men. She knew Bruce was thinking deeply about what she said and she knew he was assessing what his position was on each of these issues.

Greta then took the lead again outlining the position Little Mac felt they should take on each issue.

1. The National Debt Calculator had hit $13 Trillion with no end in sight. By the time of the election it would reach almost $16 Trillion. If it was not reduced it would bankrupt the United States and reduce the country's position in the world's hierarchy. It would not just drop the US to number two behind China; it would also mean that the United States would no longer be considered a world power. The debt must not be allowed to continue and it must be reduced. Greta knew Little Mac had an idea how to solve the problem but it was so revolutionary that he had not shared it with anyone. When the time was right they would lay out the plan to Bruce alone.

2. The war in Afghanistan had been supported by President Obama. It cannot be won and, like Russia before it, it was time for the US to get out of Afghanistan. When Bruce is elected, all US troops will be out of Afghanistan within one year. No advisors will remain. The Taliban can have the country. It was simply not in America's best interest to remain there.

3. Immigration. It is time for a National ID Card. Everyone currently living in the US would be issued one including those who are presently in the country illegally. Those who are illegal will have two years

with Government Support to obtain citizenship. They would be issued a Social Security Number with their National ID Card and would begin paying taxes immediately. No one will be allowed to do anything without showing their National ID Card. This includes boarding busses, trains, planes, renting cars, and every form of employment. Anyone without a card will be arrested and deported immediately. Any employer who hires anyone without a National ID Card will eventually, after a series of escalating fines, have their business closed by the Government.

4. Equal Rights for all. The Federal District Court in San Francisco had overturned Proposition 8 which deprived the right of marriage between people of the same sex. He would support the court's position on this issue and for the first time would come out and welcome gay men and women into the military.

5. China owns most of the debt issued by the United States. It is the fastest rising power in the world. Relations with China have been cool at best. The US must find a way to reach out to this super power, improve trade and overall relations. Bruce's relationship with the Chinese Chairman provides him a unique opportunity for discussion and trust that no other US citizen could possibly develop. It is an ace in the hole. He would travel to China to meet with his old friend, Woo Wong, during the campaign.

6. Social Security and Medicare will be bankrupt before 2025. There must be major changes to both. The baby boomers will break the bank. A new 15% rule would be enforced. A 15% reduction in benefits beginning in 2014 and a 15% increase in the amount people pay into the system.

7. Wall Street and the Financial Crisis. He would support a limit on the amount of money any person working in the United States could make in one year. The amount would be $5 million per year. This limit

would also be placed on athletes and entertainers as well as politicians and business executives.

8. It was 65 years ago when in one fiery instant the entire city of Hiroshima was destroyed. Many now believe that that should never happen again. The only way to insure it was to achieve world disarmament. He knew he would have the support of Britain, Russia and China on this issue and together they would simply have to "shove it down the throats" of everyone else. It was the right thing to do and it was the right time to do it.

Greta finished. Neither Bruce nor Jake had taken a bite of their breakfast. Their eggs were getting cold and the bacon was already so.

Finally, Bruce said, "that my dear friend is a lot to both swallow and stomach at one time. While I might have issue with some of the points made I believe it is time to broaden my thinking and venture out into the brave new world. I can live with it and sell it."

It was apparent that Bruce was excited and energized by the new thinking set forth by Little Mac. It would be a very interesting two years.

# CHAPTER 11

## PITCH AND CATCH

**Portland, OR**
**2013**

Jake sat on the bar stool talking to Toni and Mike but he never let his eye leave Bruce. Jake sat at the opposite end of the bar from Josh Morgan. Chet Linus was outside.

Over the past three years Jake had become great friends with Chet and Josh. They all had one thing in common: protect Bruce at all cost. Like Chet and Josh, Jake carried his gun in a shoulder holster under his jacket. He was an excellent marksman, had no fear and had learned to be tough and stoic. Typical Indian brave.

Bruce was smoking a cigar at the corner table with the Mayor of Portland, Bucky Myers. Bruce and Bucky were a familiar pair at the Cigar Bar. The Senior Senator from Oregon and the Mayor of Portland were good friends and seeing them together was a familiar sight to those who were regulars at Sturgis.

Jake was happy to be back in Oregon. He hated Washington, D.C. The weather sucked, the people were stuffy and way too political for him. He was, however, attached to Bruce at the hip and where ever Bruce went Jake followed.

He had called his mother earlier in the evening. She was now almost 90 years old and had lived on the Warm Spring's Indian Reservation her entire life. She was a great mom and one of the warmest and friendliest people he had ever known. Jake was her only son and he was the pride of her life. Her name was Sacajawea. She was named after the famous Lewis and Clark guide.

It was great to hear her voice and to speak to her in his native tongue. He normally made every effort to get over to see her on his return trips to Oregon with Bruce. The reservation was located just outside of Maupin, Oregon, and was an easy three and a half hour drive for him.

This time it just wasn't possible. He had flown in with Bruce on the Presidential Jet and would be here for just one night before flying out to the farthest Hawaiian Island chain in the morning.

He returned from his thoughts to his conversation with Toni. She had become a very close friend of his over the years. She was one of a kind with a mouth on her that could match any trucker word for word.

Jake loved her for what she was. She was her own person, never tried to be like anyone else. Jake knew she loved Bruce, not as much as she loved Mike, but the three were almost like siblings. There was a trust, a tolerance and a care. Each would do everything they could for each other. That's the way it had been and that's the way it would always be.

Jake loved to look at Toni and she loved to have him do it. She had the best pair of store bought tits Jake had ever seen and she loved to show them off. Mike just laughed when she flirted with Jake or when she would come to the bar dressed to kill in black leather. Needless to say the outfit was designed to show what she had to anyone who wanted to see.

Jake had never married but had a steady girlfriend in Washington, D.C. and another one in Bend, Oregon. Both were very pretty, tall and well educated. Both enjoyed the outdoors and together with Jake they made a very attractive couple.

Jake's girlfriend in Washington D.C. was Andie Johnson. Andie was an attorney like so many other people in Washington. She lived in Georgetown, like Bruce and Dorothy, but her small apartment could have fit into Dorothy's entry hall. She was an outdoor girl and every chance she had to get out and away she did. He was totally relaxed with Andie. He knew she wanted to move the relationship along but he just wasn't ready for it and, with Bruce's current job, he knew nothing would happen for at least four years.

Bend, Oregon, was home to Cheetah Rains. Cheetah was half Indian and had known Jake since they were kids growing up. Cheetah had gone to Oregon State University in Corvallis, Oregon after high school. She majored in education with the thought that at some point she would return to the Warm Springs Reservation and teach school. At this point, that career idea was on hold. She spent the Summer, Spring and Fall months as a white water fishing guide on the Deschutes River and her Winter months were spent in Bend as a ski instructor on Mt. Bachelor.

Cheetah was an adventuresome woman. She would try anything once and often convinced Jake to follow her. He finally put a stop to it after she convinced him to try tandem skydiving with her. He with his shirt off and she topless. Jake looked like a giraffe floating down from the sky and on landing his body looked like a collapsing pile of bent sticks. Cheetah just laughed at him, gave him a hug and said "well, that was interesting and kind of sexy". She paid no attention to the group on the ground that watched the spectacle occur.

She was so much like him and knew him so well that he was sure that they would be together for a long time.

He was honest with both Cheetah and Andie. He told them both that he enjoyed their company. He was not ready to choose between them and wanted them to know that each played a role in his complex life. It was clear to him that Cheetah was more comfortable with the relationship than was Andie but at least he was honest with them. He had no idea where things would end up but for now his focus was on Bruce.

Toni was watching him, waiting for the signal.

The cigar bar was packed with an eclectic group of patrons: Gay, Straight, young and old, men and woman in equal proportions. Josh sat talking with Toni, and as in the past always had one eye on him. Nothing was new tonight; nothing had changed from past nights at the Sturgis. Everyone recognized both of them but no one cared. They had been to this place many times in the past. Always the same table for a cigar and talk, then a private meeting.

Toni, Jake, Josh and Mike all watched as the two men finished their cigars and stood up. Both appeared to be heading for the rest room but when they got there they walked past and entered the Sturgis Storage Room. The bed was made up for them as it had been on many occasions in the past. Bruce liked to "pitch" and the Mayor liked to "catch." The table play made the event occur quickly. They were finished and walked back into the club in 15 minutes.

# CHAPTER 12

## DOROTHY

**Washington, D.C.**
**2011**

The campaign was in full swing and Dorothy loved every minute of being in the spotlight. She was a very beautiful woman even though she was now over 50 years old. She was well aware that her body had remained almost as it had when she first met Bruce at Stanford Law School. The cameras loved her and the press coverage she received was, at times, greater than her husband's.

She wanted to be the First Lady more than anything she had ever wanted in her life and she was determined to do what ever it took to achieve that objective.

Dorothy was born in Nebraska in 1956. Her father was Ray Ravo, founder and owner of Commercial Corn Oil Company. Commercial Corn Oil Company had become an international conglomerate over the years and was headquartered in Chicago, Illinois. The company today was known as CCOC and was listed on the New York Stock Exchange with those four letters.

Dorothy was an only child and was the pride of her father's eye. Her mother had died when she was only seven years old and, thus, she and her father were almost inseparable. She learned at a very early age how to manipulate others to get what she wanted.

She was her dad's baby and she could do no wrong. She was provided with everything her heart desired. She attended a private grade and high school and then completed her undergraduate work at Bryn Mawr College.

Her roommate's name was Brit Tiffany. Brit was very attractive as well. She grew up in New York and was sent to Bryn Mawr by her parents whom felt she needed more structure and less men. Brit liked everything about boys and was not happy about attending Bryn Mawr.

As it so happens, Dorothy and Brit realized immediately that they liked the same things and together they were able to keep a ready supply of men on hand that could service their every need.

During her junior year at Bryn Mawr, after a night of dinking, Dorothy was approached by another female student, Daisy Lewis. Daisy was more than attracted to Dorothy, and unlike Dorothy, preferred woman over men.

Both women had been drinking straight vodka for over two hours and both were well on their way to passing out when Daisy made her move. It began with a hug, then a kiss, then a hand on a breast. It didn't go much farther than that, however, as Dorothy didn't like it and was not about to experience it. That was as close to a gay relationship that she had ever experienced and she vowed that it would not happen again. She frankly couldn't understand what people of the same sex saw in each other.

She told Brit about it, and like most people, Brit was curious. "What did it feel like?" After Dorothy told Brit, she was turned off by it as well.

Dorothy was selected as a Mistress of the College and was elected to the role by the student body. This put her in charge of running traditions. There are four major traditions at Bryn Mawr. They are Parade Night, which takes place on the first night of the academic year; Lantern Night, which takes place in late October; Hell Week, which takes place in mid-February; and May Day, which takes place on the Sunday after classes end in the spring semester.

Over the course of her four years at Bryn Mawr, Dorothy managed all of the events. All were very well organized, and went off without a "hitch." Little did the college know that Dorothy had hired and paid for professional party planners to help her insure that the events all went perfectly.

Besides being attractive, Dorothy was smart. Bryn Mawr was more fun to her than work. She and Brit stayed busy on campus and, between the two of them, continued to find fertile soil outside the campus. No real relationships developed for them as undergraduates but their needs were always satisfied.

Both girls had all of the money one would ever need. Money was never an object. Their clothes were the best, designed to fit them perfectly. They were able to go to any events they desired, any restaurants they wanted to and, for that matter, anything else that suited their fancy, they simply did.

The two of them often made the trip back to New York, always stopping to see Brit's parents, but their primary mission was shopping and shop they did. Dorothy loved jewelry and never failed to bring home something new on each of these trips.

Undergraduate school went quickly and all of a sudden they were both looking at their senior year and trying to decide what to do next. Both had had enough of an all women school so the number one priority was to find a graduate school with men.

Dorothy was interested in politics and law so she finally decided she would apply to law school. Stanford and Harvard were both on her list, as was, Chicago and Michigan. She made applications to all of them. To help the application process along, her father made contributions to each law school in her mother's name.

Brit decided she wanted to go to business school and the University of Chicago MBA, program was her first and only choice.

Dorothy was accepted to, and chose, Stanford. Brit was accepted into the MBA program at the University of Chicago.

Dorothy had only been to California once and that was a business trip with her father. San Francisco was their destination and she saw and did everything San Francisco had to offer. She loved it. It was in the Fall and the weather was fantastic in the City by the Bay.

She met Bruce late in her first year of law school. She had watched him for a number of months and then took the initiative to meet him for coffee. She then asked him out on a date and, finally, to show him what she had and that she knew how to use it.

The rest was history. They were married in Chicago, both graduated on time, passed the bar and headed to Oregon to live and work.

Their early years together were great fun. Bruce was smart and actively involved in all kinds of civic and political issues. He was an absolute stud. He was able and always willing to satisfy her every need, needs that came often.

The couple never had children, neither wanted them. They, however, had a dog. It looked like a dust mop and spent half its day barking or, rather, chirping as Bruce would call it. The other half of the day was spent on Dorothy's lap. The dog's name was Petite Crêpe. The name was French and Dorothy picked it because of her love for French food; crêpes being her favorite. So the name translated to small crepe. Bruce's translation, which he often repeated, was "pile of crap" or "crap" for short. The dog didn't like Bruce and Bruce didn't like the dog. Dorothy took the "pile of crap" with her everywhere she went. The dog could actually fit in her purse and rode there often. It drove Bruce crazy.

As the years went on, Dorothy noticed Bruce had less interest in her and that her needs were simply not being adequately met. She solved the problem with the pool boy who took care of their pool and grounds at the Charbonneau home. With Bruce often in Washington the opportunity for satisfaction was at her "beck and call". Just like it was with everything else she ever wanted.

While they seemed to move farther and farther apart in the area of sexual satisfaction, they were on the same page when it came to politics. As the Senior Senator's wife from Oregon,

Dorothy performed perfectly. She loved this role, no longer needed Bruce for sex and the two seemed to gradually begin living separate lives. Their public life, however, was not that way at all. They were viewed as happily married, the perfect public servants. They were extremely popular.

She called Brit often and used her as a sounding board on almost every issue, including the pool boy.

Dorothy's dad died of a massive heart attack when she was 55. As his only child, she inherited a vast fortune, including a role on the Board of Directors of his corporation.

The current political campaign required that she resign from that corporate board in order to insure neutrality when it came to any business issue that might surface. The company was in great hands with its new Chief Executive Officer, Brit Tiffany.

It was in law school that Dorothy was introduced to two of Bruce's best friends. Woo Wong from China and Patrick O'Callaghan. Both had been his roommates at USF and the three had lived together for the first two years of their college lives.

Dorothy loved Woo, found him to be one of the most interesting people she had ever known. Woo had a charisma about him that she just couldn't put her finger on. Patrick was just ok as far as Dorothy was concerned. She was not into religion of any kind, and of late, had spent a lot of time thinking how she would deal with that subject as the President's wife. Seemed like Presidents were always thanking God for one thing or another. She didn't even know if God existed and, if God did exist, what would the world think when they found out she was a woman? Dorothy smiled at the thought.

She tolerated Patrick because of Bruce, but that was the extent of their relationship.

The campaign was picking up speed and Dorothy had started preparing herself for the questions that would be asked by reporters. She knew that each First Lady had had a special cause which they had devoted time to in the White House. She recalled the following area's of emphasis:

| Betty Ford | Awareness on Addiction – Equal Rights – Pro choice |
| Roslyn Carter | Equal Rights for all and Mental Illness |
| Nancy Regan | Just say no to drugs |
| Barbara Bush | Universal Literacy |
| Hilary Clinton | National Health Program – Foster care improvement |
| Laura Bush | Reading in the classroom, Nationwide Literacy and Better Education |
| Michele Obama | "Let's Move." Healthy diet and lifestyle for children |

Dorothy had never had children and had no interest in them. It was a tired subject and she wasn't interested in anything that had to do with children.

She liked what Michele had done, she hated fat people and the thought of being overweight just did not sync with her still perfect body, but repeating what Michele had done was not acceptable. She needed something that had more than USA appeal only. Finally, it dawned on her. When she was asked "Mrs. Gavin, as First Lady of the United States, what would you emphasize as an important issue or cause that you would devote time and effort to?"

Her response would be "Thank you for this important question. As some of you know, I have established a foundation that focuses on the importance of world wide health and nutrition. Many of the children of the world go hungry every day, are starving or are in need of the most basic of nutrients to survive. This is a cause that I have devoted much time to already and it is one that will be my cause, not just now, but for life".

Once she repeated the answer a few times and it became practiced and natural, she called her attorney and trust fund manager, John O'Brien, and told him, "get a foundation established. Use about $10 million to fund it. Call it the Food for Tots Foundation. Then, John, figure out a few people to give donations to in the USA and throughout, the world. Make it look like we have been doing this forever."

When she got off the phone she simply smiled knowing that she had again laid out a strategy which would prove her to be successful in meeting her goal.

This had nothing to do with world health. It had everything to do with Dorothy.

# CHAPTER 13

## UPPERCLASSMEN

**Shanghai, China
1976**

Woo's talk had been the perfect blend of information and humor. He was sure that following his speech that all 500 students at Shanghai Jiao would give their right arm for an American hot dog. He was amazed at the number of questions and the final applause that he received when the session ended. The talk was not difficult for him, the words flowed freely, he was not nervous and the crowd was fascinated with what he said. There was no question in anyone's mind that Woo Wong had the God-given talents of a major leader.

Phat Phing was impressed. His new friend had made him look like the second smartest guy in the room. Everyone marveled at how he was able to find such a great speaker on a topic that so many were interested in. The thanks and compliments went on for days.

Over dinner that evening Phat explained to Woo that he had decided to do one semester abroad and had settled on USF. He would do it during the winter of the following year. Phat explained that he had already applied and been accepted and that he hoped that their new relationship would continue to grow while he was in the US. Woo told him that he would make sure it would and, if he needed a place to stay, he was welcome to room with him for the semester he was in San

Francisco. Little did they know, at this point, that they would go on to become life long friends and major players in the Chinese Government.

Phat put Woo on the train back to Beijing the next morning. Both satisfied that the trip had been well worth the effort.

He treasured the remaining month he had with his mother. He made sure that he was with her at all times when she was not at work. They played tourist while he was home, had long discussions regarding national politics and world affairs. They spent many nights out at local Chinese restaurants the like of which one could not find in the United States, even in Chinatown. He ate the things he had grown up with and, for the time being, had forgotten about the junk food he had existed on during the first two years of college.

The time passed quickly and the day was upon them. Woo's flight would leave in the morning for San Francisco. He would not return until graduation. They had agreed that she would not attend his graduation. The cost would have broken their budgets. This saddened Woo but he understood that all of her sacrifice was for him and her reward would be realized when she looked at his dilpoma.

Their parting was not traumatic for either of them. They had enjoyed a wonderful couple of months together, had exhausted about every topic a mother and son could discuss, and the time was right to go their separate ways.

The flight was on time. The first, and only, stop was Hawaii and the final destination was reached on time when the plane touched down on the tarmac at San Francisco International Airport.

Woo, Patrick and Bruce had decided to live apart beginning with their third year. Patrick found a one bedroom dorm on campus, Bruce settled for a small flat in the Richmond District and Woo opted for a small apartment above a Chinese restaurant on Grant Street in the heart of Chinatown.

This time, his arrival was a bit more special than the first time he hailed a cab and directed it to USF. This time he was met with open arms by Ming Tai. It was a greeting he would never forget. He would remember it forever as the warmest greeting he had ever known.

She took him directly to his new apartment above the Chinese restaurant where they unpacked his things, shopped in Chinatown for the things he needed and made love together until they fell asleep in each others arms. What a homecoming!

Bruce had selected a flat off of 20th Avenue. It was between Geary and Anza in the middle of the block. He could easily ride his bike to campus and liked the neighborhood. It had a healthy mix of Chinese and Russians. There were lots of shops, restaurants and bars and it was only two blocks from Golden Gate Park. Bruce was not much for decorating and did not have a woman in his life, so his apartment was not what one would call chic.

He was proud of his yellow blow up chair, the two bean bag chairs he had purchased at Cost Plus and the lava lights that he put on either side of the bed. Other than that, and an old desk he had bought at a garage sale; that was it. He did not have a car but he did have his bike which he carried up and down the 25 stairs to his flat daily.

Patrick had the smallest place of the three. It was a one bedroom dorm room with a small bathroom and a partial kitchen. It was on campus so he had access to everything he needed and he knew every bus line in the city and where most of the bathhouses were.

Patrick had resolved himself to believe that sex with men was a completely acceptable way to remain celibate and, in turn, allow him to pursue his career with the Catholic Church without guilt or remorse.

Of the three, it was Bruce who struggled with his own sexuality. He enjoyed women, had made love to them during his first two years at USF, but he had also enjoyed a couple of visits to bathhouses where, for the first time, he had been excited by a man. It was something he thought about a lot but decided that this was not an issue he needed to resolve now. It was San Francisco and the 70's, whatever happened happened.

It was not long after the beginning of his third year at USF that Bruce found himself living and breathing the University from morning to night. If he wasn't studying then he was involved in some student activity that required his presence. As Vice President of the Student Body he was active in most events that involved the University. He became very familiar with the inner-workings of the University. He individually met all of the Trustees and gradually put himself in a position to become the USF Student Body President in his senior year. Bruce loved this phase of his college career. His academic performance was exceptional, his classes were not difficult for him and he loved the politics of the University.

One day while walking to his office at the Student Union, he passed by the gym and popped in to watch the USF Basketball team practice. USF was best known for its basketball program and the men's basketball team won three national titles: the 1949 NIT under Pete Newell and the 1955 and 1956 NCAA championship. The latter two were under Coach Phil Woolpert and led by player and National Collegiate Basketball Hall of Famer, Bill Russell.

Bruce was well aware that now, in the 70's, USF had retained its status as a basketball powerhouse and he was interested to watch the team as they prepared for their upcoming season.

As he sat on the bleachers and watched the team move through their drills one player stood out among the others. He was an American Indian. Bruce had read about him. He was two years younger than Bruce and had grown up on the Warm Springs Indian Reservation just outside Maupin, Oregon. Bruce was quite familiar with the area.

Practice had ended while Bruce was still sitting in the stands. He decided to use this as an opportunity to introduce himself to a fellow Oregonian.

Patrick lived on campus and was very focused on his religious studies. By his third year, he had made the decision to devote his life to Christ. He was immersed in his studies about World Religion but never lost focus on his Catholic faith. His goal was to attend the seminary immediately following graduation.

Patrick had done his homework and knew where he intended to apply upon graduation.

He had selected the Dominican House of Studies which was located on Michigan Ave, in Washington D.C. It was directly across from the Catholic University of America and part of Northeastern Washington, D.C. once known as Little Rome.

Patrick chose it in part because of its history and its commitment to graduate theological education. The building, which is Gothic style, was built in 1905 and is rumored to be the oldest poured, concrete building in the District of Columbia.

Patrick had learned that the school has a small student enrollment and a favorable faculty to student ratio. Additionally, the Thomistic theological tradition is the foundation on which Catholic teaching is based.

Patrick knew that the road ahead would not be easy and that there were many steps ahead. He also knew that aspiring priests fell, by the score, from the path before him.

He had completed just a couple of steps thus far and would soon complete the next by finishing his undergraduate degree in Religious Studies from a Catholic University in good standing. Upon finishing college he knew that he would need to make the decision that this is what he wanted to do and, if so, attending the seminary was the next step.

The seminary experience would be an additional four years. Four years in the seminary would lead to a position as a Deacon, which would lead to his taking his vows of Priesthood.

It was the 1970's, sexual freedom was in full swing, and while he had heard rumors of Catholic priest abuse of children, he had little knowledge of what that meant. If it meant the wonderful learning experience that Father O'Riley had taught him about how to remain celibate, he certainly didn't see that as a form of child abuse. In fact, he wished every child could experience what he had learned from Father O'Riley.

Patrick had learned that the Vatican was clearly opposed to homosexuality and if one was discovered to be sexually active, he could be banished from the Church.

Patrick just did not believe that his method of preserving

his celibacy was wrong or not in keeping with the vows he would some day take. He certainly did not see himself as a homosexual.

The undergraduate years sailed by, too fast for all three of them. They maintained their lasting friendship throughout the four years and managed to maintain their commitment to each other to have dinner together at least monthly.

Woo kept his promise to Phat and offered him the opportunity to stay with him in Chinatown while he attended USF for his second semester.

Phat was thrilled with the opportunity before him and, like Woo, had never been on an airplane before his flight to San Francisco. Phat was a student of military tactics and history. He was most interested in Pearl Harbor and the Japanese attack during World War II. As a result, Phat scheduled his trip to allow for a three day stay in Hawaii before going on to San Francisco. He had one thing in mind, see Pearl Harbor, understand the significance of the facility in terms of strategic importance to the Pacific Theater and learn everything about why the Japanese chose to attack the United States on this front.

He arrived in San Francisco on time and was so happy to see his new friend Woo smiling and waiting for him.

# CHAPTER 14

## THE CAMPAIGN BEGINS

**Washington, D.C.**
**2010**

Greta Hunter called the meeting to order at 9 AM. It was a cold winter morning in Washington, D.C. but the weather did not detour any in the group from being present and punctual.

In the room were Jake Rappaho, Sally Overman, Mac Foster, Lilly Langoon, John Swift, Pete Morgan, and Michael Iron, Chairman of the Republican Party. Together they represented the Directors that would design, manage and carry out Senator Bruce Gavin's campaign to defeat Barack Obama for the position of President of the United States. The election would take place in November of 2012. President Obama was in his first term as the 44th President of the United States of America.

This was a detailed strategy meeting that would provide each of the department heads with the key issues and overall strategy. Each would be required to meet with their respective staffs and, draft for review and discussion, a detailed and defined strategy for his respective area of responsibility.

After perfunctory greetings and a smattering of small talk, Greta told the group that this would be a unique campaign. The major positions they would advance would sometimes be completely at odds with traditional Republican points of view and would, most likely, cause some in the Party to not support the effort.

Greta noted that a great deal of thought had gone into the campaign already and that, thanks to Little Mac, a strategy for each major issue had been developed. She thanked Michael Iron for his support and that of the Party. She wanted the group to know that this was an all or nothing race and that everything was on the line. Michael would surely run into a buzz saw with the far right wing of the Republican Party and all were well aware that failure would cost him his job. Indeed, the same was true for virtually everyone in the room.

We know this, the 50 state strategy was designed to appeal to the needs, opinions and desires of the common working person. Those who were interested in a continued war or additional government spending would not be attracted to the strategy. Greta indicated that the positions that the campaign would take would be designed to beat Obama on his own ground and with the very people who got him elected.

She then turned to Lilly and Gretchen, and said, "this strategy means neither of you will have a break for the next two years. You will have to insure that we have covered every single state and everyone in it. This will be a "grass roots" effort the likes of which neither Party has ever undertaken."

She then looked at Pete Morgan. "Pete" she said, "we need Bruce to campaign in every state in the country. Schedule a minimum of three visits each over the next two years. Bruce is on board, so's his wife and they are both committed to it. Have at it and good luck."

She then called on Mac Foster. "Mac, would you please take the group though the major issues outlined and the strategy we have developed for each."

Though Mac stood, it still looked like he was sitting down.

He addressed the group and began by saying that with the help of some of those in the room, his policy group had been able to boil the key campaign points into eight categories. Some overlap but, in essence, they had been divided so each would get the focus and attention of the electorate. "There is no real priority to the issues outlined other than the first would be the major "hammer" point that would stand out in the minds of the

American people as a major issue that must be addressed. The state and the groups addressed will determine the priorities."

"The first and overriding issue was the National Debt. It's currently $13 Trillion and is rising at the rate of $3.2 million per minute. It will be $15 trillion by the time of the election. If it's not reversed, it will bankrupt America and reduce the country's position in the World."

"The second is the war in Afghanistan. It is now Obama's war. It can't be won and it's time for the U.S. to end our involvement in Afghanistan. Bruce's position will require all troops to be totally out of Afghanistan within one year of his election."

Mac continued, "Immigration is the next key issue. Bruce will call for a National ID card for everyone currently living in the United States, including those who are presently in the country illegally. Illegal's will have two years, with government support, to obtain citizenship. They will be issued a Social Security Number with their National ID Card and will begin paying taxes immediately. No one will be allowed to do anything without showing their National ID Card. This includes boarding busses, trains, planes, renting cars, and every job. Anyone without a Card will be arrested and deported immediately. Employers who hire anyone without a National ID Card will be sharply penalized by the Government."

Mac paused for a moment, then said, "The California Supreme Court has overturned Proposition 8 which banned marriage between people of the same sex. The Senator would support the court's position on this issue, and will welcome gay men and women into the military." The effect of this comment created some obvious discomfort around the big table. Before people could protest, Mac continued in a slightly louder voice.

"China damn near owns the United States. It is the fastest rising power in the world. Relations with China have been cool at best. We have to find a way to improve that relationship and improve trade and overall relations. Bruce's relationship with the Chinese Chairman provides him a unique opportunity for trust and serious discussions that no other political figure could possibly develop. Bruce will fly to China to meet with his old friend, Woo Wong, during the campaign."

Mac next addressed entitlement programs. "Social Security and Medicare will be bankrupt before 2025. There must be major changes to both. The influx of baby boomers will break the bank. The Senator will introduce a new 15% rule. A 15% reduction in benefits beginning in 2014 and a 15% increase in the amount people pay into the system." Again, concern in the room was palpable as the twin, nearly sacrosanct; entitlement programs were laid on the table.

Again, Mac continued in the face of shifting chairs and looks of consternation. "Next, we must address the gross mismanagement and stupidity of how Wall Street works. Bruce will support a limit on the amount of money any person working in the United States can make in one year. The amount would be $5 million. This limit will also be placed on athletes and entertainers, as well as, lobbyists and corporate executives. The facility for enacting the limit will be a 99% prohibitive tax on income, from any source, over $5,000,000."

Hands shot up all over the room and a single voice declared, "That's unconstitutional!" "So what?" Mac said. "Let me finish, I've got more."

Mac gave them time to settle down before he raised the next issue that would go against so many things the Party had upheld in the past. "Sixty five years ago, the entire city of Hiroshima was destroyed. There is a greater nuclear threat today than ever before. We must eliminate that threat and the only way to do that is to achieve world disarmament. We know we will have the support of Britain, Russia and China on this issue and together we will have to 'shove it down the throats' of everyone else. It is the right thing to do and now is the right time, maybe the only time, to do it. "

The group was silent for what seemed to be a long time but it was probably a total of 15 seconds until Sally raised her hand. "Yes, Sally" Mac said.

"Mac let me see if I get it. Please don't take my comments personally, but I have to build a communication strategy around each of these and some of them are just flat out opposite of the things we have preached in other campaigns. So here is how I boil it down."

"The National Debt leads the list and we will attack it on all fronts. We will need to have specific points raised on how we intend to deal with this and how we will approach it. I noticed that you had not come forward with any attack strategy in this area in your remarks. Obviously, "Hatchet" can do most anything but I don't think even he can cut through this issue."

Jake just smiled and said, "the lady has a good point."

"Second, we have John McCain and a whole bunch of Republican Hawks saying put more resources into Afghanistan and we are going to go against all of them and say we are getting out. Let the Taliban take it; we just don't care. Let the country continue to practice its discrimination policies against women, education and children. It isn't our problem, so we are getting out."

"Third, the immigration National ID Card makes lots of sense and that one I can clearly communicate and win both Democrats and Republicans alike. If there is a single issue that I think we can get all to agree on it is that. I think that you have a winner there!"

"Fourth, I believe that both men and women should have equal rights when it comes to marriage and I happen to be happy that this law was overturned as unconstitutional. But, having said that, the people of California passed the law and the heartland of this country just doesn't get the gay issue. The Senator has always managed to oppose this issue and now he is going to do a complete "flip flop" and support it. This is one of those Wow issues. What did he just say? I think that is exactly the opposite of what he said when I last voted for him."

"Fifth, I agree that China is an immerging World Power and on the brink of replacing the United States at the top of the list. I also agree that from everything I read they are owning more and more of our debt and we have been unable to demonstrate any means of reducing our dependence on them. I also agree that relations between the two countries have grown worse, first under Bush and now under Obama. I think I can make some "hay" on this issue but there are things that make this a terribly difficult situation."

"Six, Entitlements. We all know that Social Security and Medicare are going under but for the last 25 years no one has been willing to deal with it. Perhaps it is because it is going to "piss off" about three quarters of the people in the United States. A 1% reduction would be almost impossible to sell and you're telling me we are going for the I5/15 strategy."

"Seven, now to the income issue. Let me try to understand. We are a democracy and have been a nation that has built itself on individual drive and initiative. We have always encouraged entrepreneurial risk and accepted the outcome, either good or bad, that comes with it. It seems on the surface that limiting income at the $5 million level is going to raise a lot of concern on the part of the Republican Party we have always relied on for support. I'm not sure it is saleable to anyone. And, I don't think it's constitutional."

"Eight, well, who can argue with World Disarmament? This one I think we can easily sell if we encourage domestic use of nuclear power and don't come across as getting rid of all things nuclear."

Sally continued, "Greta indicated that our positions would be very different than those we have taken in the past. I would go farther to say, we appear to be a zebra that has gone into the rest room and changed the color of its stripes, or removed them all together."

"It just so happens, I'm in your camp on all of these issues but defining our communication strategy in the next week is a major effort. I simply can't bring up the things that have helped us win in the past and spit them out. This is new ground and is going to take a new approach." "Before I attempt the effort, I would like to know if the Senator really is on board with these points."

As if on queue, the door opened and in walked the Senator and his wife. "Jake told me you were in the middle of a spirited discussion regarding our position on the major issues we have decided to pursue during this campaign. Is that right?"

The group all nodded. The Senator then said the following, "Let me make this clear to all of you. Mind you, I didn't say perfectly clear, because there is nothing perfect about the solutions we propose but they are designed to get at the issue and bring us the support we need to win this campaign."

"We can't tolerate the National Debt. If it continues and we continue to print money to soften its blow, it is only a matter of a few years until it knocks us out."

"I am personally sick of watching American Service Men and Women die for a cause that I can't even explain. Russia lost there and we are losing. I don't think we can change the culture and I don't believe all this crap about how the Taliban are going to invade us if we don't stop them there. Let them have it! We need to get out and stop the drain on our resources and deaths to our troops."

"I love the idea of a National ID Card. Everyone in this country wins. We also start to collect taxes from illegals and if everything goes right in two years we will no longer have any illegal immigrants in this country. I think the strategy is brilliant."

"I have watched the issue of gay, lesbian and transgender surface over and over for the past 15 years. Frankly, Dorothy and I have discussed this on many occasions. I have a great deal more tolerance for the issue than she does, although, we have agreed to support it as the right thing to do for all Americans. I simply don't care what people do in their private lives. As long as they are law abiding citizens in good standing, I don't see why they should continue to be discriminated against. Yes, politically this is not the position I have taken in the past but this is the way I have personally felt. One might say "I'm coming out on this issue."

"As you know Woo Wong, the Chinese Premier, and I were college roommates and have been great friends for the past 25 or 30 years. We have been over this issue many times and both agree that if our two countries worked better and more closely together; the world would be better off for it. I know this is true and I know that we need help to accomplish what we want to do with this country. China is a major player in helping us achieve our objectives and I will see to it that the relationship is maximized toward this end."

"My generation is the straw that will 'break the camel's back' on both Social Security and Medicare. A major change is required now, not over the next 10 years. All Americans below the age of 50 will be left out of the system when it breaks. We simply can't do that to our children and our plan is reasonable and can work. It may not solve all of the long-term issues but it will certainly go a long way toward helping with the current situation and give us time for further repairs to a broken system before we have a broken promise that could cause riots in this country."

"I'm personally sick of listening to the folks on Wall Street tell the world how it is so important to pay $20 million bonuses to their key people. How many times have we heard if we don't pay, then they will leave? Where the hell are they going to go? I don't frankly understand how a 17 year old high school athlete can sign a contract with a professional basketball team for $56 million. In most cases they can't drink yet, most have a hard time talking so you can understand them and some can't even drive a car. I have nothing against them achieving success, but the excesses have to stop. I love to watch good entertainment but it needs to be affordable to all. In the beginning you could go to a Vaudeville show for a nickel. Now you have to pay 75 bucks or more for a ticket to a concert. It's time to roll this crap back and do what you need to have the entertainers roped in on how much they make."

"Last, Obama has talked forever about reducing our dependence on oil. He has supported nuclear power, solar power and wind power as alternatives along with clean coal. I want to see us support that strategy but to go one step further. No more military use of, or research about, how to use this weapon of mass destruction. It is time for the world to disarm."

Bruce then stopped. Looked at the group and said "Are there

any questions? If not, I hope that I have made myself clear. I appreciate your support on my behalf and on the positions we have decided to take." With that he turned and he and Dorothy left the room.

# CHAPTER 15

## IN HER OWN WORDS

**San Francisco, CA**
**1978**
**"A Letter to Ching"**

For me it has been the two most memorable years of my life. I do love him beyond anything I can imagine but, as we have openly discussed, all good things must come to an end and we both know that the water between us and the cultures that we have accepted will never allow us to grow old as one.

There is an old Chinese proverb that says "A child's life is like a piece of paper on which every person leaves a mark". In my case, this is very true. Woo Wong has left a mark on my life that can never be erased.

It has been two full years since we met and began a relationship and it is very hard for me to accept that tomorrow he will board a plane back to his home in Beijing and begin into the rest of his life without me.

There is another proverb that I learned from my grandfather. He said to me, "A bird does not sing because it has an answer, it sings because it has a song". We have been living with a song for two full years knowing that at the end of it there would be no answer.

Where do I begin? I guess at the beginning. I am telling you this because it is the only way I will get through this as he would want; strong and determined, like his mother, Fu Wong.

I joined the International Students Association at the end of my freshman year at USF. I did it because I thought I could help those attending from foreign countries adapt to the University, the city and the country. For the most part I have found that my efforts in that regard have proved to be very personally rewarding.

Woo Wong had assumed a leadership role in the organization by the time I had joined. To this day I have never met anyone, a man or woman, who has the natural leadership skills that he possesses. He is calm, caring, understanding and, yet, capable of making tough decisions. He has the ability to gather support for the things he believes in and he has a wonderful tolerance and interest in other points of view, even if they differ from his own.

Our relationship was slow to develop, and a bit awkward in the beginning; but, after we had the opportunity to know each other, it just took off and, in my words, overwhelmed us both.

With the exception of one semester in the middle of his junior year, we have done everything together. While we do not live together, I would honestly have to say we might as well have, as I have awakened in the morning far more with my head on his pillow than on my own.

We have never had an argument or a disagreement about anything. Go figure in today's world, with all of the pressures from all the things we go through as college students, to think I would find in this vast open space, a person who just fit; didn't try to force his way into anything. He just fit.

Sure, there have been other boys in my life. Some I have actually taken home and introduced to my parents but there has never been anyone like Woo. Woo has had total respect from my Mother and Father since the day he entered my life. He relates to them like a son. He understands the culture from which they came and enjoys the opportunity to discuss with them how the culture has changed over the years and what it is like today.

Will they miss him like I will? The answer is, yes! Do they understand why the two of us will never be able to make a life together? The answer is, yes! Will they look at me and say "Ming Tai you are wasting your time with Woo?" The answer is, no! We have all learned from him; values that will live with me for the rest of my life.

I have learned to care and respect the friends he has developed at USF. Bruce and Patrick are both special to him and I have grown to enjoy each over the past two years. Bruce and Woo are "two peas in a pod." They are focused on the same objectives and, in my opinion, they both have the capacity to make a huge difference to their respective countries.

The semester that we were, to some extent, separated occurred when Woo's Chinese friend Phat Phing arrived from China to do a semester abroad at USF. Woo had offered to share his room with Phat for that semester and, as such, it changed the pattern the two of us had grown accustomed to.

Woo's apartment was small and positioned over a restaurant in the heart of Chinatown. Phat loved it because he awoke and went to sleep with the sounds and smells of home. He slept on a couch for almost four months. He never complained. He was neat and orderly and very respectful of Woo and, for that matter, me.

Phat was a very interesting guy and very different than Woo. There was an edge about him that I couldn't get my hands around. He was very focused and definitely a Communist at heart. He loved military strategy and would spend hours at the library focused on military history and the strategies used by countries to either win wars or peacefully expand their power.

Phat was a very different guy than Woo. He seemed to be on a mission as opposed to Woo who was very patient and looked at years as small steps in the learning process. Woo would say, "Be patient Phat, all things will evolve over time but in order for them to meet the objective desired, the ground work must be laid. The soil must be tilled for the crop to grow."

I felt like we spent that semester as tour guides. I'm not sure how I got so involved but Woo wanted me to be there and what he wanted, I did.

Phat left China for his study abroad at USF just after Deng Xiaoping was reinstated as a Vice Premier and, shortly, before Deng was appointed as Vice Chairman of the CCP.

By the time he returned to China most of the conflict had subsided. The Radicals led by Jiang Qing and her Gang of Four had been defeated. In fact, the final showdown between the radicals and moderates occurred in 1976 following the death of Zhou Enlai. On April 5th, at a spontaneous mass demonstration held in Tiananmen Square in Beijing to memorialize Zhou, Mao's closet associates were openly criticized. The authorities forcibly suppressed the demonstration which was considered a vote for support of Deng.

It was clear that Phat was a moderate, he was not a radical and he did not support Mao. I was never sure why, but I got the feeling from Woo that Mao's actions had significantly impacted Phat's family and, for that, he would never forgive them.

In any event, once Phat had completed his semester studies abroad at USF, he boarded a plane for Shanghai and returned to his studies at Shanghai Jiao Tong University.

I will remember Phat as a moment in time. He seemed to relate to Woo, but was a very distant guy to the rest of us. Bruce, Patrick and I tried, but just couldn't relate to him.

There have been so many memorable moments over the past two years; some serious, many not. One of my favorite moments was when I introduced my mother and father to Bruce's best friend. His name is Jake Rappaho. Jake was from Oregon like Bruce. He was recruited by USF to play basketball for two reasons: the first was he was good; and the second, he was 6'7" tall. Jake is an American Indian. To begin with you don't find a lot of American Indians in Chinatown and you see no one who is 6'7".

My parents had invited Woo and his friends to a celebration dinner in honor of the Chinese New Year. It was 1976, the year of the Dragon.

The dinner was set for New Year's Eve and the group invited

would all have prime seats from the balcony of my parents home for the parade. The meal was homemade and traditional Chinese.

The guests as I recall were Bruce, Patrick, Jake, Woo and myself.

Jake was the last to arrive. When he walked into my parent's home, he created quite a stir. To both of my parents, Jake looked like a giant. He was so tall he could not stand up straight in any room in the house. The poor guy had to sit down the entire night until we went out on the balcony to view the parade.

My mom, just stared. She didn't say anything. I knew, however, that as a woman, forget the fact that she was Chinese, she was trying to visualize body parts. And no matter how hard her mind tried she just couldn't imagine. It still makes me laugh today. She even asked him his shoe size!

The dinner that night was another giggle for me. My mom cooked traditional Chinese fare. All of the food was fantastic and both Woo and I enjoyed it from start to finish; it was a real treat. The boys, however, were not so sure and each in their own way, should I say, "danced around their plates." As I recall the menu consisted of the following:

Stinky Tofu. The Chinese name for this is Chou Dofu. It is a brine made with shrimp, vegetables and salt that is fermented for months. Then you soak tofu in it for several hours. Woo and I loved it. The very smell to the others was hard to take. To Jake's credit he tried it. My mother loved him for it.

Sea Cucumber. We have this in all of our Chinese medicine shops. It looks like a chunk of cement in the display cases. It is the dried form of sea cucumber also known as beche de mer. Basically it is an ocean creature that looks like a cucumber but has tube feet and a ring of tentacles around its mouth. The actual taste is bland. Both Bruce and Patrick got through his one far easier than they did the Stinky Tofu.

Mom also served as an hors d'oeuvre, Thousand Year Old Eggs, which are preserved eggs. They are made by preserving duck eggs in ash and salt for one hundred days. This turns the white of the egg a dark gray color and gives the eggs an ancient appearance. They have a strong salt flavor. Jake 10 points. Bruce and Patrick 2 points, in my mom's scoring book.

Last, I remember the Bird Nest Soup. The chief ingredient is the Swiftlet which is a tiny bid that lives in the caves in Southeast Asia. Instead of twigs and straw, the Swiftlet makes a nest from its own saliva. It is the only bird in the world to do so. Harvesting the nests requires real skill. The taste is rather bland to me but to the boys credit they all said they enjoyed it. Truth be known, I think Woo was the only one telling the truth.

In any event I remember the evening as a special one. Mom and Dad hosting Woo and his best friends with me along for the ride.

Making love to Woo was an experience way beyond my years. It was natural, comfortable, easy and gentle. It was as though we had lived a life together and knew just what was needed by each of us to make each time special and seem like the first time. I wonder if I will ever have the same experience again.

Woo continued to grow at USF in leaps and bounds. He was the leader of the International Student Association, and he played a major role in the politics of the University. He was elected Vice President of the Student Body in our senior year. He ran with Bruce as a team. Bruce was elected Student Body President that year and together they were an unstoppable force within the University.

Never have I been so proud to be with someone as I was that final year with Woo.

But my dear friend, "all good things must come to an end," and so we have come to this point. In two days, Woo will leave the United States to rejoin his family and begin his career in China.

My parents had him to dinner last night and, believe me, all of us cried our eyes out. They will miss him dearly as will I. We, however, were all open to the reasons that this was more than a departure. We are miles apart in culture. Not so far apart in values, but the traditions and political history of the Chinese are the primary reasons my family is here in San Francisco and I was born in San Francisco.

Last night we laid together again. I don't think either of us slept a wink. We didn't cry, we actually laughed a lot. At times the bed just shook. Not from exciting love but from reliving our many moments together. What a lot of laughs.

Tomorrow, I will take him to the airport for the last time. Tonight will be a special night for both of us. Tomorrow night will be the emptiest night of my life. I'm still not sure how I'm going to deal with it, but I will. I know this has been a wonderful experience.

I've decided not to think about tomorrow. I will live the rest of today and tonight with all of the energy I can muster. We will go out on a high note together. We will look up, not down! We will each move forward but, sadly, not together.

So Ching, you have been my best friend since we were born in the same hospital in Chinatown, on the same day, of the same month, of the same year, just two hours apart. I needed to get this out, I appreciate your taking the time and listening quietly to my story. It has been a wonderful trip. Thanks.

# CHAPTER 16

## THE TREE PEONY

**San Francisco, CA
1978**

The Tree Peony, known as "Mudan" in Chinese, has been grown as an ornamental plant since the Sui Dynasty, or perhaps earlier. The Sui Dynasty stretched from 581 to 618. China does not have a national flower but, if it did, most believe that it would be the Tree Peony.

Tree Peonies have a growth cycle that is very different from other plants. As the Chinese saying goes, "Grow the above ground parts in the Spring, doze off in the Summer, grow roots in the Fall, and go to sleep in the Winter." The process is slow. The plant does not just spring into life but rather takes its time. It takes Tree Peonies at least five to eight years of growth to stabilize the flower.

Such was the case with Woo Wong. His growth and development were slow and calculated. He was patient, knowing when to rest. He also knew when to move ahead at full speed.

By the time Woo had reached his Senior Year at the University of San Francisco, he had already planned his next growth stage.

The Cultural Revolution in China was over and the education system was one of its beneficiaries. China was in the process of modernizing its educational system. At the time, Woo was ready for his next step the Masters in Business Degree was virtually unknown in China.

The government, for the first time, began to invest in education, a process that has been ongoing since the end of the Cultural Revolution.

During the Cultural Revolution between 1966 and 1976, higher education suffered tremendous losses, the system was almost shut down and much of a generation of college and graduate students, academics and technicians, professionals and teachers, were lost.

Woo was about to return to his country, ready to pursue his graduate education in a land where, as a result of the cultural revolution, there was a huge void in trained talent to meet the needs of society.

However, the pragmatic approach of Deng Xiaoping, recognized that to meet the goals of modernization, it was essential to develop science, technology and intellectual resources and to raise the population's educational level. That population had reached one billion and China needed an educated workforce to meet the needs of its society.

Woo had watched all of this change while he had spent four years away at USF. He was ready to return and he knew where he wanted to study.

He applied to Graduate School, majoring in Business with a minor in Political Science at Shanghai Jiao Tong University in Shanghai. His academic history was outstanding and he immediately received confirmation of his acceptance.

As he sat in the plane on the runway at San Francisco International Airport he tried to picture his last year at USF and in the United States. To Woo, it seemed now to be a huge blur. He had experienced and achieved so much. He was elected Vice President of the Student Body, graduated with highest honors, and, of course, had fallen deeply in love with his constant companion, Ming Tai.

He knew she was still standing in the airport staring out the window at his China Airlines airplane. She probably had a tear in her eye, but so many had been shed over the past two months that it was hard to believe there were any left to release.

She had been his rock, his love, his companion for the last two years. Her family had sustained and nurtured him and would have his unwavering respect forever. Woo, Ming and her family, were all in agreement that the relationship had been wonderful. As good as it was, though, it had to end, and they all understood that as well. He knew, as he took his seat on China Airlines Flight 566, that the end had come.

That reality was slowly sinking in and came home when the engines roared; the airplane moved swiftly down the runway and, suddenly, lifted off. The airplane rose quickly and slowly turned out over the Golden Gate Bridge and headed directly west. A final tear dropped from his eye and he had the emptiest feeling he would ever experience.

The next stage of his growth had begun.

The airplane arrived slightly late in Beijing and, his mother, Fu Wong, was waiting with the largest smile on her face. In her hand, she held a bouquet of flowers. They were the traditional flowers of China. They were Tree Peonies.

After a long hug, she gave him the flower bouquet. He then presented her with a special gift. He asked her to open it, now, at the airport. He did not want her to wait.

She unwrapped the package and looked at the framed certificate.

It said "This certificate of graduation is presented by the Trustees of the University of San Francisco to Woo Wong. Mr. Wong has graduated this date in June 1978 with the highest honors this institution can bestow on a graduate. Mr. Wong is to be commended for his outstanding academic performance."

A tear appeared in Fu's eye. She had worked so hard and waited so long for this moment and she knew then that all of her efforts had been worthwhile.

Woo entered Shanghai Jiao Tong University in the Fall. His roommate was his old friend, Phat Phing. Phat had completed his undergraduate degree at Shanghai Jiao Tong and his acceptance into the Graduate Program was an automatic, given his strong academic performance.

Woo focused on business and politics. Phat studied engineering and military history. Both were involved in politics within the university and for the first time outside the university setting.

The Communist Party of China (CPC), also know as the Chinese Communist Party, is the founding, and ruling political Party, of the People's Republic of China. It is the world's largest political Party.

Deng Xiaoping was now leading the Party and brought back all of the state apparatus' that had been dismantled during the Cultural Revolution. The Party's highest body is the National Congress which meets at least once every five years. The primary organization of power in the Party is detailed in the Party constitution, and consists of: the central committee, which includes the Politburo Standing Committee with its nine members. The full Politburo has 24 full members. The Secretariat, is the principal administrative mechanism of the CPC and it is headed by the General Secretary of the Communist Party of China. The remaining piece of the Central Committee is the Military Commission, a parallel organization of the government institution of the same name; the Central Discipline Inspection Commission, charged with rooting out corruption and malfeasance among Party cadres; and the Other Central Organizations, including the General Office, the Central Organization Department, the Propaganda Department, the International Liaison Department and the United Front Department. There are, in addition, numerous commissions and groups.

Every five years the Communist Party holds a National Congress. The Congress serves two functions. It approves changes to the Party Constitution regarding policy and it elects the Central Committee. The Central Committee, in turn, elects the Politburo.

The Party's central focus of power is the Politburo Standing Committee. There are two other key organs of political power in China: the Formal Government and the People's Liberation Army.

***********************

**Beijing, China**
**1988**


Phat Phing was most interested in the military and in rooting out corruption within the Party. Phat, after one year, was selected to be a member of the Central Advisory Committee. A committee assignment could mean future appointment to the actual Central Discipline Inspection Commission.

Woo was far more interested in the Government and, particularly, the Central Political and Legislative Affairs Committee. After one year, Woo was selected to participate as a member of the Central Political and Legislative Affairs Committee.

Time passed quickly for both young men. Graduate school was easy for them. Each found that the subjects they had selected were the right ones, and because of that, school was interesting and positive results came.

Graduation occurred for both after two years. The question of a doctorate degree crossed the minds of both of them but by the end of graduate school, each was very involved in the Communist Party and it was now taking the majority of their time and attention.

After three years of working within the lower Party committees Phat and Woo had moved up.

Woo was living in Beijing where he had grown up and Phat remained in Shanghai. They kept in touch, but on an infrequent basis. Each was following his area of interest and their two paths did not often cross.

By the time he was 32, Woo Wong was Chairman of the Central Political and Legislative Affairs Committee. He had moved up over the years from the advisory capacity to eventual

123

appointment on the actual committee and now was its Chairman. He clearly understood the Party and how it operated. He had set a goal for himself that, by the age of 40, he would be the youngest member of the Politburo.

Like Woo, Phat was active in the Party, and while he was a couple of steps behind Woo, he was climbing the ladder. He had achieved significant status as a member of the Commission for Protection of Party Secrets.

Both Woo and Phat had more education than 85% of the senior party officials. They were both extremely intelligent, which propelled them forward, but also created jealousy among those who saw them as a "steam train about to run over everything in front of them."

# CHAPTER 17

## PART 1

### NORA NOITALL

**Portland, OR**
**1988**

Nora Noitall was an investigative reporter for the Portland Oregonian. Prior to moving to Portland, she worked on the I-Team at Channel 7 in the Bay Area. The I-Team did investigative reporting. It was an "in your face" approach to controversial subjects and issues. Most of the I-Team leads came from the general population and most proved to be very interesting.

Nora moved to Portland from San Francisco to "get a greener life". She was single. Living in the City of San Francisco and working for the I-Team had her career going absolutely nowhere. The rent for her studio took three quarters of her monthly check, severely limiting her social life.

She loved the Pacific Northwest and when the opportunity came available to join the Oregonian Staff as an investigative reporter she jumped on it.

Nora worked on a wide variety of stories for the paper and, after three years in Portland, she felt very comfortable. She had a very nice two bedroom apartment on West 23rd just off Burnside. Her apartment was not far from the Pearl District and, on nice days, which she would say were very limited, she would walk down the hill to shop and browse in the numerous art and antique stores that now covered the area.

Her apartment was about two blocks off Burnside. The District had numerous coffee shops and great restaurants, most of which she frequented on a regular basis.

Since moving to Portland, even her social life had picked up. She had a steady boyfriend who was doing his internship at the University of Oregon Medical School and when they had time to be together, it was always fun.

Nora hated her last name. It was pronounced "No E Tall" but, as one would guess, everyone pronounced it "NO IT All" which did not serve a reporter well. Over the years she had learned to ignore it but there was hardly a day that went by that someone didn't bring it up.

She didn't mind the rain and what seemed like constant overcast. She loved the outdoors and with two great rivers and hundreds of streams, plus Mt. Hood, she always had something to do.

Her boyfriend was John Thomas. John had grown up in Portland, graduated from the University of Oregon in Pre-Med, and was now in medical school in Portland. John's parents had a cabin on Mt. Hood, on Road 29, which she and John had full use of. The cabin was like so many others on Mt. Hood, it stood on Forest Service Land but had a 99 year lease. The only drawback was that the cabins on Forest service land could not be occupied full time; they needed to be used for vacation and recreational purposes only. This worked well for both John and Nora but not so well for John's parents. Because of the forest service rule, the bad guys knew that the cabin would be vacant and, thus, all of them were the targets of break-ins and thefts.

It wasn't too many years after John's parents purchased it that they decided the cabin would be the most sparsely decorated cabin on Road 12. To that end, they made sure that the furnishings in it would not be items that anyone would want for free.

The cabin was on Still Creek. In Oregon, they pronounce "creek" as "crick" which Nora thought did the locals no good.

In her estimation they came off sounding like a bunch of backwoods hicks.

The cabin still took its water from the "crick" and it had no indoor bathroom facility. When you had to go, it was outside in the outhouse, or to the nearest tree depending on your sex and the urgency of your need.

John and Nora loved it. The nights by the fire with a good Oregon Pinot Noir were some of the best times she had ever experienced.

Shortly after her third anniversary with the Oregonian, Nora was asked to look into land use fraud on the Warm Springs Indian Reservation.

Nora was aware that Native Americans had to fight just to get ownership of land they were promised years ago. What she didn't know is that the problem still existed today.

Historically, Native Americans have had a much higher appreciation for the land and, what it can provide them. They attach a spiritual component to the land and, as a result, they approach the relinquishment or sale of those lands with great trepidation.

What Nora had been told was that there was a controversy brewing over a portion of the Deschutes River that ran through the Warm Springs Indian Reservation. In the original land grant it was clear that the Indian nation had rights and owned the river to its center and that anyone using the river required a land use permit issued by the Reservation.

In recent years, the State of Oregon, pressured by the Department of Fish and Game, the whitewater rafting lobby and the towns of Bend, Redmond, and Maupin had come together to lobby for river use without permits. They further argued that the river had changed course over the years and the portion of the river that was originally granted to the Indian's, now occupied dry land on the south side of the Reservation.

It didn't take Nora long to realize that the local and national legislatures were becoming less willing to afford Native Americans the protections to which they had become accustomed. In Oregon, there was legislation pending that would, in essence, rewrite a portion of the original Indian Reservation treaty to allow for public use of Indian land, specifically, the Indians portion of the Deschutes River.

Nora learned that a first term congressman from Eugene had taken up the cause on behalf of the Warm Spring Indian tribe. His name was Bruce Gavin.

Nora had never heard of Bruce Gavin, but she intended to meet him and discover everything she could about this issue. As a person devoted to the outdoors, she didn't like the smell of this from the moment she was given the assignment. She had to remind herself that she was a neutral investigative reporter but she found herself already siding with the Indians.

Nora made an appointment with Congressman Gavin to meet with him in his office in Salem. She phoned his office and he picked up the phone himself. "Bruce Gavin, can I help you?"

After a brief introduction, Nora made an appointment with him. She was amazed how easy going and friendly he was. He seemed serious about the issue and indicated he thought that the Tribe was once again "getting screwed." He was so frank on the phone that she immediately found him totally refreshing. The appointment was set two weeks in advance.

During that time, she studied this issue and learned that Native Americans were still being taken advantage of to this day. What little portion of land they had been permitted to inhabit by the U.S. Government was now being reacquired for use as toxic waste sites, recreational and even development uses. It was clear that the Indian nations had no real representation within the US Government. They were in need of a strong and powerful voice and some influential groups or individuals to assist them with their strategies.

Nora felt that perhaps Bruce Gavin was one "white man" who was willing "to step up to the plate" on their behalf.

It was clear to her from her research that the United States must acknowledge past treaties and let the Indians manage their lives and lands free from harmful influences and inroads on their uses of their own land.

While researching the issue, she came across a bill signed by President Clinton on Indian Sacred Sites. In the bill, the President articulated his position that each Executive Branch with responsibility for Federal lands management must allow Native Americans full access to these sites for religious purposes and avoid altering the physical makeup of these locations. He mandated that Federal access to these lands be restricted to achieve this objective. Nora thought about what she had read. Something had triggered this issue and brought it up to the President's attention. She filed away this related issue for future reference.

The two weeks passed quickly. Prior to her meeting, she had done quite a bit of homework including making the drive over Mt. Hood to the Warm Springs Reservation. To her delight, she also found, on Indian land, the Kah Nee Ta Hot Springs and, before she left that day, she managed to spend a full hour soaking away.

Kah Nee Ta High Desert Hot Springs was located on the Warm Springs Indian Reservation. It was first started by a non-Indian doctor who owned land around the hot springs of the Warm Springs River. In 1961, the Tribes purchased the land back and started to rebuild the spa. Nora was surprised to find a full resort and casino on the property as well as a historic lodge.

Her stay at the Reservation was brief but very informative. She went to the Visitors' Information Center, showed her press pass, and asked if she could be directed to someone on the Reservation who might have knowledge of the history of the place. She was directed to an old woman who lived down a long, dusty road in a small cabin that overlooked the Deschutes River. Her name was Sacajawea.

On the day of the appointment, Nora drove I-5 down to Salem. Her appointment with Congressman Gavin was scheduled for 10:00 AM and she prided herself for being on time and prepared for the discussion. She knocked on his door at precisely 10:00 AM.

The door opened and she was greeted by a very attractive,

well built, man who introduced himself as Bruce Gavin. She was invited into the office and was introduced to a giant of a man whose name was Jake Rappaho. Nora was trying to remember if she had ever met a man this big. He was obviously an American Indian. Nora was sure he was right off the Reservation and probably wouldn't speak much. In addition, Bruce introduced her to Cheetah Rains.

Cheetah could have come straight off the cover of some outdoor magazine. She was not only beautiful, but had muscles that seemed to line every part of her body. She was not weathered in appearance but clearly had spent the vast amount of her time outdoors. She had no idea what nationality Cheetah was but she obviously wasn't a white woman who spent a lot of time indoors.

After they sat, Jake spoke first and said, "Good morning Ms. 'No E Tall'." Nora almost fell off her chair. Not only was this monster attractive, he was articulate, and right out of the box, he pronounced her name correctly.

"We appreciate your coming to meet with us today. We know you are a reporter with the Oregonian and that you've been assigned to cover the dispute involving the Warm Springs Tribes and the land that they were given." "We also know you've visited the reservation and met with one of the tribe's elders."

Nora nodded and said, "yes, I met with a very wise, old woman, whose name was Sacajawea."

Jake responded matter-of-factly "Sacajawea is my mother. I grew up on the Reservation, as did Cheetah."

Nora then looked at Bruce and said, "It is my understanding, Congressman, that you have taken an interest in this issue. Can you tell me what you've learned?"

Bruce replied. "I have known Jake and Cheetah for over 10 years. There are no people alive that I trust more than them. If they say there is a problem here, I believe them. From what I have seen and learned, I believe that there is a movement afoot to take land that was lawfully transferred to the tribe by treaty." "Let's hear from Jake and Cheetah. Cheetah, why don't you start."

"Thanks Bruce. A quick bit of history, over one hundred years ago, a U.S. treaty gave three tribes the rights to more than 1,000 square miles of land. That land is known today as the Warm Springs Indian Reservation. You've seen it, so I don't need to describe it, but one of the boundaries described in the treaty gave the Indian Nation ownership of a portion of the land on which the Deschutes River runs today. I believe it states that the Nation owns to the middle of the river on the side that the Reservation is located."

"Over the years, the Indian Nation has profited from this by requiring that anyone using the river, either for recreational or business use, must have a permit and a license to operate. That may not sound like a big deal but on average, for more than nine months per year, there are over 150 boats daily that utilize these waters."

"Directly across from the Reservation is what looks to be vacant land for as far as the eye can see. That land is not vacant but is used to graze cattle. It is a small part of the largest ranch in the State of Oregon. That land is the crux of the current dispute."

"That land is owned by a rancher named Hank Simon. You may have heard of the Bar S Ranch. That is Mr. Simon's ranch. Mr. Simon doesn't just run cattle. He owns more than half of Maupin, the town nearest to Warm Springs. He owns the entire town of Sisters, Oregon, and the land on which it was built, and he has significant investments in Bend. He runs numerous businesses from each of those towns that utilize this portion of the Deschutes River. For a number of years Mr. Simon paid the fees required to properly license his rafts, boats, fishing, and hunting guide services. Five years ago he stopped paying and began a slow process of ignoring the Indian requirements while lobbying the State Government and its legislators to return the river to the people of Oregon. He has maintained that the "Red Nation" has been holding the good people of Oregon hostage for far too many years and it needs to stop."

"Just to put it in perspective, the annual fees that Mr. Simon has refused to pay amount to more than $500,000 per year.

In our estimation, he owes the Indian nation more than $2.5 million for past use."

"My people don't have the resources to fight this issue. At one point we asked the Land, Forest, and Fish & Game Service to check permits of those using the river. It was only a matter of months before we learned that they had all been paid off and we have not seen an agent on the river for more than four and a half years."

"A local group of Indian men tried to begin to check boats themselves but, on more than one occasion, they have been fired on with rifles by those using the river. We do not have proof but we believe they are Mr. Simon's men."

"We brought this problem to Bruce's attention and, with some digging, Bruce has been able to learn that there is a significant amount of lobbying going on to pass a bill that would allow for public non-fee use of the Deschutes River." "This, in our opinion, is nothing more than a land grab and a reduction in the rights that were given to our people more than 100 years ago."

"So, Nora, that is the problem we face. We know that a bill is already in draft form and that the legislature may address this as an issue beginning in the fall session. It is already the middle of July. We have no money to lobby with, we have limited legal representation and we believe that we are about to once again be screwed by the United States Government."

Nora had been writing furiously during Cheetah's soliloquy. There was no question in her mind that this was a real issue and, from what she had read prior to the meeting, this appeared to be just one more example of Indian abuse.

She looked at Jake, Bruce and Cheetah and said, "You make a very compelling case and I intend to look into it myself. I want to understand Mr. Simon and the Bar S Ranch. I also want to know how, and by what means, he is getting away with what appears to be outright fraud. I have a very powerful tool behind me and when I feel it is appropriate to use, I will, and it is amazing what the power of the press can do. I may have to call on each of you to help. I hope I can count on your continued candor."

After the group assured her of their willingness to assist, Nora thanked them for their time and support.

# CHAPTER 18

## PART 2

## THE INVESTIGATION

**Portland, OR**
**1988**

Nora's mind was awash with thoughts about what she had learned from Jake, Cheetah and Bruce in Salem. Her years as an investigative reporter told her that she could be on to something big. It was the feeling of the chase that thrilled her about her job. She had learned over the years that her profession was not an easy one and, with it, came a danger that more often than not was very real.

She arrived at the paper's downtown headquarters and immediately went up to her desk. First item on the list was to learn everything she possibly could about Mr. Hank Simon and the Bar S Ranch.

She found several articles and references to Mr. Simon, his family, and his business dealings. Mr. Hank Simon was the son of Buzz and Rachel Simon. They had ranched in Eastern Oregon for over 50 years. When both passed away, the ranch, and all of the holdings, passed on to Hank. He expanded the herd of Black Angus cattle to its current level. No one knows for sure, but the herd is estimated to be over 100,000 head. To operate the ranch, he has a staff of over 100 men. His foreman's name was Willy Johnson and, rumor has it, Mr. Johnson was not a very nice man.

According to newspaper articles, Mr. Johnson is totally loyal to Mr. Simon and has been for 20 years. He is known to have a huge temper and likes to beat the hell out of staff. In fact, Bar S cowhands have been known to just disappear.

Mr. Simon's non-ranch operations were run from an office complex in Bend, Oregon. Ms. Jennifer Lopez was his business manager and like Mr. Johnson, Ms. Lopez ran all of the non-ranch operations with an iron fist.

It was Ms. Lopez who controlled the political purse strings and it was Ms. Lopez who could often be seen wining and dining the Oregon legislators in Salem and Portland. She was tough, and sexy. According to the articles she came across in newspaper gossip columns; it appeared that Ms. Lopez did not own a blouse that had less than a 12 inch "V" neckline in the front.

As near as Nora could tell, the two Bar S operations worked separately, unless an issue brought them together. It looked like the Reservation land issue was one that brought them together, with Ms. Lopez leading the legislative charge, and Mr. Johnson providing the river muscle.

Nora was also able to learn that Mr. Simon was very rarely seen in public and, to get access to him, or to try to access the ranch, was almost impossible.

Nora spent the next two weeks developing her plan of action and then she called Cheetah and setup a meeting at the Visitors Center. Cheetah was a very experienced river guide and looked forward to both the discussion and a whitewater trip down the Deschutes.

It was a bright summer day in Eastern Oregon. The temperature was around 88 degrees and promised to get hotter as the day progressed. Nora was dressed in a tank top and shorts with tennis shoes on. Cheetah might as well not have had anything on. Her top was very loose fitting, wearing no bra under it. Her cut off jeans could not have been shorter. She wore her standard "get wet" sandals. Anyone looking at her would think she had picked the sexiest outfit in her closet to wear but, the simple fact was, she could put anything on and people would look.

Cheetah was naturally brown skinned but, with the time, she spent outside, she was nearly black. She was the perfect outdoor woman, tall, beautiful, muscular and smart. Like Jake, she had been born and raised on the Reservation and still maintained a small cabin there.

The trip down the river was uneventful but provided Nora with the picture she needed in her head to move ahead with her plan. During the trip she brought Cheetah up to speed on her plan and, at the same time, asked for her help. Part of the plan involved one of her good friends, Susan Knight, who was an attorney in Portland. Nora would need the tribe's permission to hire Susan to represent them.

Prior to making the trip, Nora had visited the Oregonian Press Pool and met with one of the photographers whose name was Jack Samuels. Jack was an easy going guy who didn't shy away from any assignment. Nora explained to Jack the situation and that if he wanted to be a part of her team, it could mean that he might find himself in danger, to the point where he could be hurt, or possibly, even killed. Jack just smiled and said "Baby I'm yours. Take me away".

Over a beer, sitting on the porch of her small cottage on the Reservation, Nora explained the plan in greater detail to Cheetah. Cheetah would make sure that she briefed both Jake and Bruce.

The plan was to work the investigation on two different fronts. Nora explained what she had learned about Hank Simon, and his operation, including his enforcer Foreman Willy Johnson. She also explained the business and lobbying operation that was run by Ms. Jennifer Lopez.

The plan was fairly simple. Nora and her friend, Susan, would spend a couple of Friday and Saturday nights hanging out in a bar in Maupin called "The Cattleman's Watering Hole". Their goal would be to meet some of the men that worked on the Bar S and get to know them to the point that they could use them to get a message into the Bar S and the ears of both Hank Simon and Willie Johnson. The message would be simple, the girls had learned that the Indians were planning to reactivate their "search and intercept" mission on the Deschutes and start enforcing the treaty law themselves.

At the same time, Jack had agreed to start checking in with the fishing and rafting shops in Bend, Maupin and Sisters, explaining to anyone he could find that he was from the Federal Department of Fish & Game and he was giving the shops advance notice that they have been identified as sponsors of trips taken on the river without Indian permits. He told them that the Department has decided to enforce the regulation and that, if they did not comply, they would be fined $500 for every trip that resulted from a booking at their shop that did not have appropriate Indian licenses.

Nora went on to explain that she and Susan, as well as Jack, would make it clear that both the Indian search operation and the license inspection would commence on August 15th.

It would also be on August 15th that Jake and his look alike Indian crew, comprised of Nora, Susan, Cheetah and Jack, would begin to search vessels, knowing that one of them would be filled with Willy's men from the Bar S Ranch. Jack's camera would do the rest of the work.

On the other front, Bruce would spend enough time getting to know the three legislators that represented the area from Mount Hood to Bend. The three legislators were the ones pushing for the bill's approval. At the same time, Bruce would be getting to know Ms. Lopez, with the idea of being able to hear her pitch. With a little luck, Jack's lenses would again do the work.

Nora explained that while she still didn't have solid evidence, she was sure the three legislators representing Eastern Oregon were on the payroll of the Bar S Ranch in some form. She had checked out each of their homes. They were not homes that could be supported on a legislature's meager salary. Nora would investigate each of them herself over the next couple of weeks.

The overall goal would be to obtain enough evidence to support a case against Mr. Simon and the Bar S Ranch, obtaining damages that would exceed the fees owed to the Reservation. At the same time, Susan felt, that in addition to fees owed, there should be additional punitive damages that would go to the tribe. Nora then went on to say that, in addition, she wanted to make sure that the appropriate Indian licensing operations were reinstituted within the companies who make their living off the river, and lastly, and perhaps most important, she noted that it would be a pleasure to watch three Eastern Oregon legislators be dumped by the public they were supposed to represent.

The Cattleman's Watering Hole proved to be the ideal spot for both Susan and Nora to pass on the gossip they had created. Susan and Nora had met in Portland at a bar where they were both playing pool against a large group of guys who simply couldn't beat either of them. From that evening on, their relationship had grown, and now in this dusty tavern in Maupin, Oregon, dressed in their finest cowgirl attire, they took on all comers at the pool table. In the three nights they worked the room, they guessed they had met about 30 of the cowhands that worked on the Bar S Ranch. They probably fended off 20 moves, drank more beer than they had in an entire year, and won quite a bit of money. Some of the cowboys made innovative moves; others were tired and worn out. Obviously, neither of the girls had any interest. They were on a mission to lead the cowboys down a very thought through path. Both Susan and Nora were sure that the August date registered in most of the guys' minds and that news of the pending Indian action would make its way back to Willie and Mr. Simon.

Jack was in his element. He had posed as a federal agent of the Forest Service that was looking into local officials at Fish & Game who were not enforcing Federal law. He managed to scare the life out of about 50 merchants over the course of two weeks and he was sure the word had drifted back to both the local Fish and Wildlife guys who were on the take and the Bar S Ranch. Then he spent the rest of his time with his camera.

Nora had not had time to do everything herself, so she hired a private detective to look into the background, lifestyle, and bank accounts of the three legislators from Eastern Oregon. John Jacobs represented the Maupin District. Ellen Fries represented the Bend District and Eric Whitehouse represented the Redmond area. The findings of the private detective would make for wonderful reading. He not only had monitored their bank accounts, but had proof of deposits made to their accounts that traced back to Mr. Simon's company in Bend, Oregon.

Bruce did his part as well. He made sure that he met and got to know Ellen, John and Eric and let them know that he was interested in the issue and open to discussion about how to free up land and water for the use of everyone in Oregon. It wasn't long before he got a call from Jennifer Lopez. She introduced herself, and indicated that she was working on behalf of the group supporting the Freeing of the Wild River for the Benefit of Public Use. She booked a dinner with Bruce to discuss it.

She arrived at the agreed upon restaurant in a dress so low-cut as to leave no doubt that this wasn't a routine business meeting. He had done his homework. She had not. If she had, she would have known that Bruce lived with the best pair of tits money could buy, and by any standard of comparison, Ms. Lopez couldn't compare. Besides, Bruce wasn't there to ogle her decolletage . He was setting a trap.

He left the dinner with the clear understanding that, if he was supportive of the position when the votes came in the Fall, he would be greatly rewarded for his efforts in ways that would benefit him both financially and, if he desired, sexually. Little did Jennifer know that Bruce had recorded the conversation and that money, like her tits, was not important to him.

In the meantime, Jack, the photographer, had been busy. He had staked out each Congressman and, over the course of two weeks, had an enormous array of photos of each of them with not only Willy, but with Mr. Simon himself.

On August 15th they launched their high speed river raft and headed out into the Deschutes to begin checking permits. The process went well until a big boat rounded the bend. Jack saw it first and started taking lots of pictures. The first gunshot just missed the bow of the boat. The second hit Jake in the arm. He fell back into the boat and blood started to flow everywhere. Susan and Nora tended to Jake while Cheetah cranked up the motor and headed away towards the Indian side of the river and safety. The shooting continued for some time. It was returned by Jack in the form of camera clicks. With his high speed lenses he had more than enough direct hits to sink the boat, everyone in it and everyone who supported it. Two of the men in the boat had their Bar S hats on and the name on the logo on the front of the boat was Bar S. The plan worked perfectly, with the exception of Jake being wounded.

Within three weeks everything came together. Nora was itching to break the story but she and Susan both knew a number of things needed to happen before she let the "dog out of the house." First, Susan wanted Federal indictments against the three legislators and, at the same time, she wanted support for the charges she intended to bring against Mr. Simon, Willy and Jennifer Lopez. Next, she wanted an arrest warrant for Mr. Simon and Willy charging them with attempted murder, fraud, theft and racketeering.

The day came. The Headline read: "RANCHER ACCUSED OF ATTEMPTED MURDER AND FRAUD AGAINST THE WARM SPRINGS INDIAN TRIBES". Below the headline was a smaller one that said: "Three Oregon State Congressmen Linked to the Charge."

After a long winter, numerous motions, and trial, it was finally over. The verdicts were all in favor of the Indian Nation. The results brought great joy to Nora and Susan.

Mr. Simon and Willy were guilty as charged on all counts, minimum jail time of 25 years for each; ten year terms for the ranch hands that participated; ten million dollars in restitution made to the Warm Springs tribes for income lost and punitive damages. All three congressmen were found guilty of conspiracy, removed from office, and were forced to give up their homes. Without the Bar S bribe support, they simply could not afford to live. Jennifer Lopez - guilty of conspiracy to defraud the Indian Nation - five years in Federal Prison.

The stories ran on an ongoing basis from September until conclusion in March. Nora received the credit she deserved and Susan's career took a huge leap forward.

Bruce and his wife, Dorothy, threw a huge celebration party on the Willamette River for the Indian Nation. Sacagajea, Cheetah, and Jake were all present as well as other Indian dignitaries. Nora and Susan were the stars of the evening and shared guest of honor privileges.

It was a clear Spring night on the river, as the guests filed out, no one had any idea, that, as fate would have it, Nora would cross paths with the Gavins again in the future.

# CHAPTER 19

## A BRIEF ENCOUNTER

**San Francisco, CA**
**1978**

There was one week left before they were to graduate from the University of San Francisco.

They had all talked about graduation and all planned to walk, as opposed to "skip" the graduation ceremony, and have the certificate sent to their home. Hard to believe but more and more students were choosing to go the non-walk route rather than don the cap and gown in traditional fashion.

Bruce thought it would be a great idea to bring the group together one last time before they all went their separate ways. It was a Friday night and each had been given a suggested dish to bring to Bruce's flat.

First to arrive was Woo Wong and his girlfriend Ming Tai. Woo and Ming were in charge of the main course and they had chosen Chinese chicken chow mein, fried rice and stuffed shrimp. To Bruce, it looked like Woo and Ming had brought enough to feed an army. Ming also brought fortune cookies for each to open following dinner.

Next to arrive was Patrick O'Callaghan. Patrick was in charge of dessert and had with him two huge blackberry pies and ice cream.

Jake Rappaho was the last to arrive. Jake was responsible for the appetizers. Jake was not into cooking or anything that had to do with it. He solved his part of the dinner by stopping at the Italian Deli on Folsom Street and buying two items that looked good to him. The first were mini pizza bites. Jake bought 30 of them. He then added a large Italian antipasto tray. It had olives, salami, mortadella, cheese, marinated artichokes hearts, olives and marinated vegetables.

When Bruce looked at the menu, it didn't take him long to decide that if he ever decided to do this again, it would be a good idea to have some sort of a theme for the meal.

Bruce was in charge of the wine and spirits. He had three choices for the group, white or red wine, cold beer, or vodka and gin tonics. There were also soft drinks but the only one who had one was Ming.

It was a great evening. They all relived the past two years and told one story after another. The evening passed quickly, almost too fast. Before they began to leave Ming handed each of them a fortune cookie and asked that they read theirs out loud to the group.

Bruce went first, "You are a leader among men and your skills will be rewarded."

Woo followed, "Confucius says, small men carry big sticks."

Jake opened his and read, "The strong will conquer the weak. You have the strength to make a difference."

Patrick then opened his, "The Lord blesses those who follow His direction. Make it be your guide."

Last to open was Ming, hers read, "Time passes and, with it, memories fade, both good and bad. So it will be with your life."

The fortune cookies were so appropriate to each it was as though Ming had made them up. Truth be known, she did, but never let them know it.

The first to leave was Woo and Ming, they were followed by Jake. Patrick decided to stay behind to help Bruce clean up.

Both Patrick and Bruce were pretty blitzed from all of the wine they had consumed. Their conversation continued with the stories that they could not share with Ming in the room.

Patrick talked about the numerous bathhouses he had visited over the past two years. Bruce had joined him on at least three occasions.

Patrick explained to Bruce that the bathhouses provided him with a sexual outlet. He explained that the experiences helped him insure he could maintain his celibacy for the priesthood. The thought of his being gay never entered his mind. He talked about the excitement he felt when he was exposed to other men and how it made him feel. He assumed the feeling would be the same with women but he didn't want to take the chance.

Once inside the bathhouse, he and Bruce always went their separate ways so neither knew what the other was up to. Neither Patrick nor Bruce ever discussed their bathhouse experiences so the conversation they were now having was new to both of them.

Patrick's conversation was so explicit that Bruce began to be aroused by it.

Patrick kept detailing his encounters. He talked about the house with the knot hole room. He told Bruce that the room was designed to add mystery to the sexual experience. He indicated that once aroused you would put your penis through one of the holes and whoever was on the other side of the wall could do with it as they desired. Patrick detailed the experience and the different results he had experienced with that room over the past two years.

Patrick asked Bruce what his feelings had been on the few occasions he had accompanied him to the bathhouses. Bruce replied that he was not sure. He had mixed feelings. On the one hand, he enjoyed the experiences he had had with women outside the bathhouses; and, on the other hand, he had been sexually aroused by the experiences with men when in the bathhouses. Bruce wasn't sure but thought he might be bi-sexual.

Patrick looked at him and said "what are you feeling now?" knowing that there was a bulge appearing in the crotch of Bruce's pants. Bruce said that the talk was exciting him. With that Patrick turned Bruce's head toward him and kissed him slowly and deeply.

The bedroom was located just off the kitchen. Their clothes were off in an instant. Both were very hard. Bruce "pitched" and Patrick "caught". It was over in 10 minutes.

It was, for a moment, an experience which both enjoyed but never discussed or shared with anyone again.

Graduation day was a great celebration for all of them. The two years had gone by so quickly.

# CHAPTER 20

## THE CAMPAIGN

**Washington, D.C.**
**2010**


Greta Hunter sat in her Washington office contemplating the campaign that was now underway. She was very well aware that political campaign strategies vary by candidate; but, almost everyone would agree that in order for a successful strategy to win, you need to have two things, an electable candidate and specific targeting of those who will support your candidate.

Greta knew that she had the right candidate and now was sharpening her focus on the audience she wanted to target and, in turn, to gather support from.

Barack Obama's brand created by his campaign was for the past two years designed to make the American public feel good about our government. During his first two years in office he had worked hard to keep Americans hopeful. Many felt his administration was truly one of surface, not substance. Greta recalled the words of Charlie Finley who at one time was the owner of the Oakland Athletics Major League Baseball team. Charlie once described those who wanted to purchase the A's like this, "Big hat, no cattle".

Greta felt that the Obama campaign had created an image based culture, one dominated by junk politics, communication through narratives, pictures, and carefully orchestrated spectacles.

She knew a large segment of the American public was either ignoring or didn't want to accept, that there was a completely different picture behind the current President's optimism.

His Administration had spent, lent or guaranteed $12.8 trillion in taxpayer dollars in a doomed effort to re-inflate the bubble economy. She felt this was simply a tactic that, at best, would forestall catastrophe and leave the country completely broke. She also knew her belief was shared by millions of Americans.

Greta also knew that Obama had already allocated nearly $1 trillion in defense related spending and the continuation of the doomed war in Afghanistan. Even though Obama had pulled the last fighting troops out of Iraq by the end of August, there were still 50,000 troops that would remain in Iraq for the next 15 or 20 years.

Couple these facts, with the other facts on his record, including the following:

1.  He refused to support the single payer healthcare bill, HR676, sponsored by Representatives Dennis Kucinich and John Conyers.
2.  He has continued to support the war in Afghanistan, including the use of drones sent on cross border bombing runs into Pakistan.
3.  He refused to ease restrictions so workers can organize.
4.  He has no policy on immigration and has sued the State of Arizona for trying to move something forward on this issue.
5.  He supported the death penalty.
6.  He backed a class action reform bill that was part of a large lobbying effort by financial firms.

Greta also knew that the public was beginning to show their lack of faith in his strategy. His numbers dropped in the polls each month. This was a year of mid-term elections and there were many contests up for grabs. The Democrats were on the ropes and her campaign strategy must now furnish the jab and then the knockout punch.

She had already set up her 50 state strategy and would not back off in any state, even if the Republicans had never won there. True to her plan, she had booked Senator Gavin into a minimum of three visits to every state in the Union over the next two years.

She was working with the Obama Campaign folks to hold a minimum of seven debates between Senator Gavin and President Obama. The debates were positioned like a blanket designed to completely cover the United States. The debates were scheduled for New York City; Chicago, Illinois; Austin, Texas; Palm Beach, Florida; Los Angeles, California; Kansas City, Missouri; and Honolulu, Hawaii.

Sally Overman had developed a communication strategy for the issues outlined by Bruce and Little Mac Foster. Each would hit the airways in every state in the United States. The eight issues, key to the campaign, are as follows:

1. The economy, national debt and its impact on the United States.
2. The war in Afghanistan.
3. Immigration.
4. Equal Rights, to include Gays in the Military and Gay Marriage.
5. China. Greta knew that it had just been announced that China has overtaken Japan as the second most powerful economy in the world.
6. Out of control government entitlements and spending.
7. Wall Street.
8. World disarmament and the elimination of all nuclear weapons.

The Republican Party had committed financial resources to the campaign. Bruce was not opposed on the Republican front and, even though the campaign had taken points of view that traditionally would have been unheard of in Republican circles, they were all designed to target a wide audience and one, if not more, would have appeal to everyone that heard the Senator's message. The fact was that the traditional republican point of view could not win. It was clearly demonstrated in the last Obama vs. McCain election. It was therefore hard for Greta to listen to, or tolerate, those who continued to sound off on the old way being the only way. Good old Newt Gingrich was one of those traditional voices that they completely ignored.

She felt each issue was built on a solid foundation. They would hammer these sub points and action plans home with every talk, with every press release, at every debate and in every campaign ad. She thought about how each point was made and how she would work it into the overall strategy.

Greta simplified each as follows:

**The Economy and the National Debt**

Greta knew there was much to be done on this issue. But in her discussions with Little Mac they had focused on some key areas. Little Mac had told her to stay focused on these issues during the campaign but with victory would come his idea on how to resolve this issue once and for all.

- Reduce the budgets or eliminate 150 specific identified programs.
- Focus on Medicare overspending and waste. Eliminate overpays for drugs and stop relying on drug manufactures to define prices. Estimated savings were $12.3 billion annually.
- Stop funding colleges and students. Federal student loan programs will be eliminated, $21.8 billion worth of student loans are already in default.
- Eliminate earned income tax credit overpayments. The earned income tax credit provides $31 billion in refundable tax credits to 19 million low income families. The IRS estimates that $8.5 billion to $9.9 billion of this amount is wasted in overpayments.

**The War in Afghanistan**

- The war in Afghanistan had been supported by President Obama, but now it was time to get out of Afghanistan. All US troops will be out of Afghanistan within one year. No advisors will remain. The Taliban can have the country. It was none of the US' business.

**Immigration**

- It is time for a National ID Card. Everyone currently living in the US would be issued one, including those who are presently in the country illegally. Those who are illegal will have two years, with Government support, to obtain citizenship. They would be issued a Social Security Number with their National ID Card and would begin paying taxes immediately. No one will be allowed to do anything without showing their National ID Card. This includes boarding busses, trains, planes, renting cars, and every job. Anyone without a card will be arrested and deported immediately. Any employer who hires anyone without a National ID Card will face severe penalties.

**Equal Rights for All**
- The California Supreme Court had overturned Proposition 8 in California, which deprived the right of marriage between people of the same sex. He would support the court's position on this issue and, for the first time, would come out and welcome gay men and women into the military.

**Relations with China**
- China owns the United States credit instruments. Relations with China have been cool at best. The US must find a way to reach out to this super power, improve trade and overall relations. Bruce's relationship with the Chinese Chairman provides him a unique opportunity for discussion and trust that no other US citizen could possibly develop. He would travel to China to meet with his old friend, Woo Wong, during the campaign.

**Federal Welfare Program Reform**
- Social Security and Medicare will be bankrupt before 2025. There must be major changes to both. A new 15% rule would be enforced. A 15% reduction in benefits beginning in 2014 and a 15% increase in the amount people pay into the system.

**Wall Street Reform**
- The campaign would support a limit on the amount of money any person working in the United States could make in one year. The amount would be $5 million per year. This limit would also be placed on athletes and entertainers, as well as, politicians and business executives.

**Nuclear Disarmament**
- It was 65 years ago when, in one fiery instant, the

entire city of Hiroshima was destroyed. The only way to insure it didn't happen again was to achieve world disarmament. Bruce knew he would have the support of Britain, Russia and China on this issue, and together they would simply have to "shove it down the throats" of everyone else. It was the right thing to do and it was the right time to do it.

The campaign was in full swing. Bruce was on an airplane, boat, train or bus, almost every day. Dorothy accompanied him almost everywhere he went. She was as into the campaign as he was, maybe even more so. She was tireless in her efforts to support him and had used her focus on World Hunger to attract the attention of many. Her foundation was now well known and her personal contributions to the issue were significant. Sally Overman saw to it that every man and woman living in the United States, and most of the world, knew what Bruce stood for, that he was clear on each issue and how that differed from President Obama's first two years in office.

# CHAPTER 21

## THE RISE OF WOO WONG

**Beijing, China**
**2010**

In the Fall of 2010, Woo Wong defeated incumbent Hu Jintan and was named the President of the People's Republic of China.

The title is interchangeable with the Chairman of the People's Republic of China. The incumbent is responsible to the National People's Congress and is the head of state of the People's Republic of China. The office was created by the 1982 Constitution.

It is a single candidate election whereby the candidate is recommended by the Politburo of the Communist Party of China.

Over the past 10 years Woo Wong had worked his way up through committees and then was named a member of the Politburo which consists of 24 full members of which nine are members of the Central Committee. It was not long after his appointment to the Politburo that Woo was named to the Central Committee.

Woo carried with him a reputation that he had earned along the way. He was known for being extremely smart, politically savvy, and a solid decision maker.

According to the Constitution of the People's Republic of China the National People's Congress has the power to elect and force the resignation of the President. It was the National People's Congress that requested the resignation from Hu Jintan and, in his place, elected Woo Wong.

By law, the President must be a Chinese citizen of 45 years of age or older. The President cannot serve for over two successive terms, which translates to about 10 years. The President does not have any administrative power: the position is that of a powerless figurehead.

However, the President promulgates statutes adopted by the NPC. While the functions of the President are ceremonial, the President appoints the Premier upon the decision of NPC, Vice Premiers, State Council members and Ministers of all departments upon the nomination of the Premier, all Ambassadors to foreign countries and all legislative committee chairs, treasures' and secretaries.

The President has the responsibility to give Special Presidential Decrees, and to declare a State of Emergency, and declare War ritually upon the decision of the NPC. The President is assisted by the Vice President.

Over the years, the Chinese Presidency had become a powerful post since it combines with the General Secretary, the Head of the Party. Since the 1990's it has been the general practice for the President to also serve as the General Secretary of the Communist Party of China.

However, the relationship between the President and the military is more complex. In theory, when the President is also Party General Secretary, he can command the Party Central Military Commission to order the state Central Military to act. This has not happened in the recent past and, with Woo's knowledge of how to make things work best, he would continue to foster the importance of maintaining a degree of autonomy for the People's Liberation Army.

Woo Wong was a student of the Chinese Government and knew how things got done, by whom, and when it was best to act. In any system, he was a very astute politician. While he gave a wonderful sense of friendship and ease of understanding to those he came in contact with, the reality was he knew exactly what he was doing each step of the way.

Woo had never married. He left his true love in San Francisco and the emptiness could never be filled by another. He had never forgotten Ming Tai. He had not spoken with her in years but he received a handwritten note with her love and congratulations upon his election to the Presidency. He did not respond to her but he kept the letter with his most personal belongings.

With the power of the Presidency came the power to appoint. Woo selected his long time friend and political ally, Phat Phing, to assist him as Vice President of the People's Republic of China. Phat was not married as well. He was far more sexually active than Woo had ever been, but he kept his affairs to himself and the ladies that entertained him knew full well to never open their mouths or they would not see the light of another day.

Phat Phing had been a very loyal soldier to Woo Wong throughout the years. He knew what it took to insure Woo was appointed or elected to the various positions and, on more than one occasion, made sure that any stumbling blocks were removed, even if it involved the mysterious disappearance of someone that appeared to be in Woo's way. Phat didn't discuss his actions with his friend in advance but he was sure that Woo knew who was behind his ongoing success. Both men were now in their 50's.

Phat had continued with his interest in the military and the power of the People's Liberation Army. He personally knew each of the Generals and knew as much of their responsibility as they did.

Phat was not nearly as polished as Woo. In fact he was blunt and ruthless. He frightened those who were his opponents. Those who dared to stand in his way were either moved aside or removed. Many of those that had been removed just disappeared.

Since Woo's election, the Chinese economy had heated up. By September of 2010 the Chinese economy had overtaken

Japan as the world's second largest economy after the United States. Japan's gross domestic product or GDP totaled $1.29 trillion for the three months ending in June. China's official figure for the same period was $1.34 trillion.

The International Monetary Fund had forecast that China's output would reach $5.4 trillion by the end of 2010.

The economy was growing at a breakneck pace. The average growth period in the second quarter of 2010 was 10.3%. The economy was being driven by exports; trade surplus hit an 18 month high of $28 billion in July.

There was no question in Woo's mind. He would see during his 10 year term as President that China's economy would unseat the United States as the world's largest economy.

The other thing Woo knew was that his nation was flush with cash and would use it to advance its cause worldwide when any opportunity arose.

Woo shifted his thoughts from the rosy economic forecast to the terrible tragedy that was currently happening in China's Northwestern Gansu Province. As of today, Woo had been told that over 1,117 Chinese people had been killed as a gigantic mud slide had swept the town of Zhouqu in Gannan Prefecture.

Heavy rains continued to lash the remote section of Northwestern China and the death toll was continuing to rise. Hopes were fading that additional survivors would be found.

Woo had been told by local officials that they believed at least another 700 people were missing. The total deaths could reach a number higher than the US World Trade Center attack.

Woo also knew that the National Meteorological Center had warned that there was a relatively large chance of more landslides coming in the days ahead. There simply was no end in sight for the rain. It was pounding this part of China at a rate that exceeded 3½ inches per day.

Woo had dispatched rescue teams from the Central Government and troops from the People's Liberation Army had been sent to the area.

It was a calamity beyond the abilities of even the most adept leader to repair. People were traumatized; clean drinking water was a primary concern, as was water born diseases.

Woo had been given pictures taken locally. Buildings were torn from their foundations, lower floors blown out by the force of the debris laden water. At least three villages comprising hundreds of households were entirely buried and much of the countryside in the province was submerged.

Woo had ordered crews to spray disinfectant chemicals across the ground and over machinery. Dysentery, lack of sanitation, and accumulating garbage, all joined together to make this one of the greatest disasters impacting the people of China.

Woo had been called before the Politburo to brief them on the rescue and relief work and to outline the strategy he had designed to deal with the problems.

He would address the Committee in the morning. It would be his first presentation to the Committee since his election. He was not looking forward to it as it was a dire subject and fraught with issues that neither he nor Phat could control. Phat, as Vice President, would accompany Woo to the meeting.

At 8:00 AM sharp, Woo addressed the members of the Politburo. There were exactly 35 people in the room at the Central Meeting Quarters, 25 members of the Politburo and 10 security guards.

As always, Woo was prepared. He opened the discussion with a summary of the current situation. At a minimum, approximately 2,000 Chinese citizens had lost their lives as a result of an act of Mother Nature. He outlined all of the measures that the government had taken and those that were planned. He explained what the National Weather Forecast had said and prepared the group with the thought that the worst was yet to come.

Woo was smooth as ever and had the attention of most of the Politburo. There was, however, one member of the Central Committee that was not in agreement. His name was Wi Jong. Wi was a supporter of Hu Jintan who had been asked to resign and make way for Woo Wong. Wi Jong attacked Woo at every opportunity, on every issue. Over and over he pounded in his points that Woo was slow on the draw. He faulted Woo for not providing the needed support and chided him for extending the suffering of the people of Gansu Province.

Phat sat stoically next to this boss and listened to the pounding criticism.

Wi went on to say that in order to back up his concerns with fact, he intended to visit the area personally in one week's time and would report back to the Politburo his findings. He also indicated to the group he was sure the results of his investigation would reveal the absolute lack of care and concern by the current President for the citizens of China.

Phat listened. He did not make any gestures or facial impressions. He simply listened to his boss and to the tirade of Wi Jong.

The storms did not end. The flooding continued and the situation worsened. Wi Jong did as he said. He made a tour of the impacted area.

Unfortunately, while he and two of his aids were inspecting the underside of a bridge, a wall of water came surging down the river and took all of them into the roaring river. They were found later, each had been the victim of drowning, an act of nature.

What was not evident was that all three had identical pin prick marks in their necks. Each caused by a blow dart. The darts were covered with a poison instantly lethal to man. However, there was no evidence as the darts were made of clay and designed to disintegrate when they touched water.

It was a sad day for the Politburo. Woo hosted a National Funeral for Wi and complimented him in the National Press as a real hero of the reform.

The replacement for Wi was the next major and, somewhat controversial move, by Woo. There had never been a woman on the Politburo, let alone on the Central Committee. Woo had his eyes on a woman to replace Wi.

He knew that this would be a major first for China and its citizens. He also understood from his time in America that women were not only smart but, by and large, often more focused than men at making strategic decisions.

It was 2010 and time to test the system. Woo had the woman picked out long ago and was ready to propose her to the Politburo. Her name was Xi Ling.

Xi was well educated. He had first met her at Shanghai Jiao Tong University. She was active in the International Student Association and had made a point of coming up to him after his talk to compliment him and the way he had introduced democracy to the group.

Woo had watched her as a young Communist and how she had taken active roles in committees and social actions that Chinese women would normally shy from. He was impressed with her and wanted to watch her as she grew and developed. He saw many traits in her that he had seen in Ming and, perhaps, Woo saw Ming in her and was living his dream seeing her again vicariously through Xi. Woo had always dreamed that the true love of his life would blossom into a major force in the Chinese culture. Perhaps through Xi this was going to come true.

When he made the election nomination, the Politburo reacted like a snake that was striking a rock before it knew it would only have a sore mouth with nothing to show for the strike. The National Press picked up on it and that was what Woo was counting on.

The women of China were immensely supportive. It was not a good time to try to repress their feelings and explain the ways of old China. "The cat was out of the bag" and it would never again be in it.

Wi was appreciative but she knew that Woo would have only done this if he thought she was competent and could handle it. She was and she could.

That discussion was now public and the women had won. It was over before it began. The Politburo Central Committee now had its first woman member. Most accepted the appointment; though a few would never get over it.

# CHAPTER 22

## THE ELECTION

**Washington, D.C.**
**2012**

The date was August 31, 2012. Greta sat in her Washington office. She then stood, took a deep breath, walked over to the wall, and using her black felt pen, marked another day off the giant calendar on the wall. The campaign was down to 66 days before the General Election. The General Election will be held on November 6th.

She was well aware that elections for President and Vice President of the United States are indirect elections in which voters cast ballots for a slate of electors of the U.S. Electoral College, that, in turn, directly elect the President and Vice President.

It had been a very fast two years since Bruce had agreed to run as the sole candidate on the Republican side of the ticket. Like he did in 2008, President Obama used his charismatic personality and speaking skills to combat the real issues which Bruce continued to hammer home.

In 2008, he was able to use these same skills to defeat Senator John McCain. In doing so Obama won 52% of the vote to McCain's 48%. Obama snagged 349 electoral votes in the process. Greta knew he was a fighter. The 2008 election and his victory came at the end of the longest and most interesting election in American history.

If the polls were correct, Bruce had made a real dent in the President's desire to be re-elected. Bruce was ahead in 23 states and his results were climbing every day. On a national basis, he was only six points behind Obama.

When it came to the issues developed two years ago by Little Mac, the Senator was able to score major points on the national debt issue and the past spending policies of the President. When it came to Afghanistan, it was a no contest issue. The President still supported the War and the Senator said we can't win it, it is a losing cause, it cost too much and we need to get out now.

On the issue of gay rights and gay's in the military, the Senator had lost some ground. The conservative side of the party just couldn't buy into it and Obama had refused to take a position saying he will abide by what the court decides. The issue would go before the Supreme Court of the United States some time in the future. Obviously the Senator's position would garner him the gay vote but he needed a great deal more than that to pull this election off.

The Senator had overwhelming support for his position on immigration and the national ID card. She was sure that when the Senator first mentioned that issue in their first debate that the Obama campaign wished they would have thought of it first.

As to China, no one questioned the new power in the East. General consensus was relations needed to improve.

As to the issue of nuclear disarmament, both candidates supported it and both supported continued use of nuclear power to offset the problems associated with oil.

Obama was being dragged down by two issues, the first was the economy. Jobs were not coming back fast enough for the American public and everyone was afraid of the national debt and how much every American owed the People's Republic of China. He also could not get away from Afghanistan. It was now clear, the American public wanted out of the country; the faster the better. However, the position was still challenged by the Conservative Right.

Greta would now spend the next 60 days focused on two issues. She knew that President Obama's popular vote had been dropping very quickly over the past two years and it was these issues that would either make or break Bruce.

The 50 state strategy had worked. She was not sure how they did it, but Bruce had visited all 50 states at least three times during the past two years. The road show was very effective. Town Halls were arranged at every stop and his open collar and sleeve rolled up tactics were paying big dividends.

She had to credit Dorothy as well. Dorothy had made the majority of visits with him, was very comfortable in speaking about the issues, and had developed a significant following of her own. Greta laughed to herself. Dorothy had about every "old pervert" in the US following her around. No question in Greta's mind. It was the body and how she clothed and showed it at her age.

In two hours she would again assemble the entire group of department heads for one last final meeting and then would set the 60 day strategy.

The National conventions had gone well, Senator Obama had held his one year ago in August, and Senator Gavin held his in September of that year. Coming out of the conventions most observers thought the Presidential race was close. President Obama was joined for a second term try by Vice President Joe Biden of Delaware.

Senator Gavin selected the former governor of the State of Florida, Jed Bramble. Jed Bramble was a very conservative republican. He agreed totally with Senator Gavin on every issue except the gay rights issue. He and the Senator had talked about this openly and had no problem with letting the American public know that one of them was for it and one of them was against it. On all other issues they were in total agreement.

The usual staff began to file into the conference room. Senator Gavin, his wife, Dorothy, and former Governor Bramble were present, as was Michael Iron, Chairman of the Republican Party.

Greta opened by reminding everyone that they were about

to employ their final 60-day strategy. She indicated that the last 60 days would be focused on getting out the vote. This would be particularly true at the two ends of the spectrum, those that were between the ages of 18 and 25, and those that were between the age of 70 and 80. Greta believed that these were the two groups that would make the difference in this close campaign. The younger group went for Obama in 2008 and the older group for McCain. The strategy would be to bring the groups into alignment this election with both going for Senator Gavin.

Greta looked at Lilly and said "this is your time to shine babe and I want you to pull out all stops and take no prisoners. We need to keep your eyes, ears and feet on the ground and move your teams in all 50 states to get out the vote. Millions have contributed, now we need the vote of everyone who mailed us a check, even if it was for one dollar."

"Our communication effort will be on two issues only. The economy, including the national debt, poor job growth and excessive government spending and the war in Afghanistan. We know we are winning on both of those issues and we know they top the list of the American people. We will focus intensely on both. We have made our points well on the other issues and everyone knows where we stand on all of them."

"We need not revisit the gay rights subject. Our position to have Senator Gavin for it and Governor Schrub against it had made it a neutral issue in the minds of those that care one way or another."

"We will lump the entitlement issues with the economy so we add a little more fuel to the fire."

"The Senator has one more debate with President Obama in Los Angeles in September, after that the debate season will end."

"We want the last 60 days to look highly energized and in order to convey that image we have booked the hell out of Senator and Mrs. Gavin. Pete has scheduled them 7 days a week from now until the election. As great of shape that they are both in, by the end of this 60 days of breakfasts, lunches and dinners they are both likely to look like Bubba and Bubbett Gavin."

The group laughed, that is everyone except Dorothy. She saw nothing funny about being described as a potential Bubbett.

Everyone had their marching orders. Prior to ending the meeting Greta looked at the group and said "from my own personal perspective, we owe a significant amount to each of you for the success of this campaign. Bruce called me last night and wanted me to tell you in the confines of this room, that when we are successful, and he is President of the United States of America, that everyone in this room will have a very meaningful position within his Administration. Now go get them. Thanks. "

The next 60 days moved so quickly that it didn't seem like one could differentiate one from another, they were all a blur. The debate went well in Los Angeles.

In keeping with the strategy, Senator Gavin stayed focused on the two target issues and did not let other questions deter him from making sure that the general public watching knew that the President was directly responsible for the current economy and its lack of jobs and that his position on Afghanistan was wrong. The Senator pounded on the point that to keep dumping money into a war we can't win was irresponsible.

Sally didn't miss a beat on the press coverage associated with the debate or on the whirlwind schedule that the Senator and his wife had undertaken.

The 57th quadrennial United States Presidential election was held on November 6, 2012. President Barack Obama, and his Vice President, Joe Biden, were in the fight of their life against Republican Senator Bruce Gavin from Oregon and his Vice Presidential Nominee, Senator Jeb Bramble, the former Governor of Florida.

President Obama had come to the realization over the past 60 days that the American public was fed up with the US economy, his spending habits and the National Debt. He also recognized that no matter what he said or how he said it, the American people do not want to fight or support a war in Afghanistan.

November 6, 2012 was election day in 50 states and the District of Columbia; it was the last of 21 consecutive election days in Oregon which abolished the voting booth in 1998. The majority of states allowed early voting, with all states allowing some form of absentee voting.

Voters cast votes for listed Presidential candidates but they were actually selecting their state's slate of Electoral College electors.

Obama was shocked when he lost Illinois (his home state), the Northeast and the critical battleground states of Ohio and Pennsylvania. He had won all of them in the 2008 election.

By 8:30 in the evening, Senator Gavin had won the entire Northeast by comfortable margins and the Great Lakes states of Michigan, Wisconsin and Minnesota by double digits. This was the exact opposite result that President Obama had achieved in the 2008 election.

The strategy that Little Mac and Greta had developed for the last 60 day push had taken hold. The traditional Republican states of North Dakota, South Dakota, Utah and Oklahoma all went to Senator Gavin.

The President won the states of Iowa and New Mexico and was leading in California. Senator Gavin had taken Oregon, Washington, Idaho, and Alaska. Hawaii was still voting but expected to go to the President.

By 11:00 PM Eastern time all the polls were closed on the West Coast. The major networks of CBS, ABC and NBC all called the election for Senator Gavin. He had amassed the needed Electoral College votes to defeat the sitting President.

His victory party was being held in the Benson Hotel in downtown Portland. At 10:30 PM on November 6th, President Barack Obama called the Senator to congratulate him on his victory and his well run campaign.

The entire Gavin staff was present as were a number of special invited guests. Jake had made arrangements for his mother, Sacajawea, to attend and he had reserved an entire floor at The Benson Hotel for her and the entire Warm Springs Tribal Counsel. Sacajawea had never been farther than Bend, Oregon, before and she had never stayed in a hotel that looked anything like The Benson. The Indians were in full tribal dress and they made for a uniquely interesting picture.

Nora was covering the event for the Oregonian and her friend Sue was with her. The Indians were surrounding her and it was like old home week. Brit had made the trip west to support Dorothy and to join in the celebration as well.

Off to one side of the room was Father Patrick O'Callaghan. There was something about Father O'Callaghan that caught Nora's attention. She didn't know what it was but she found herself studying him during the course of the evening. He obviously looked pleased and very proud of the Senator.

Jumping up and down in the front row was Mike and Toni. Toni was in her best pink leather outfit and her boobs were all but falling out of it. What a sight it was, talk about diversity. The cameras caught it all, from the Indians, to Toni's pink leather and Father O'Callaghan's Priest Collar. How could one man attract this mix of friends? It was a mystery to many but not to the hundreds of thousands of Americans who had voted for him.

Michael Iron was all smiles and shaking every hand he could find.

At exactly 11:30 PM West Coast time the President Elect and Dorothy appeared before a mass of supporters at the Benson Hotel. They both looked fit and ready to begin a new stage in their own lives and to keep the promises to the American people that they had made during the campaign.

President Elect Gavin kept his remarks short and to the point.

"I would first like to thank President Obama and Vice President Biden for a well run, hotly contested, campaign."

"Throughout this battle, I believe that both sides played by the rules and showed respect for each other. I am appreciative of this and want the American people to know that this election could serve as a model for the future. Both sides, in my opinion, focused on the issues at hand, openly debated often, made their respective points and differences known, and let the American people decide what and who they wanted."

"To all of you in this room and to all Americans still up and watching these remarks, I want to thank you for your support and trust. I intend to do what I said I would do in the campaign debates and I intend to begin the process now so that once I take the oath in January we will be already moving full speed ahead."

"To my wife, Dorothy, I want to say a special thank you. She has been a constant companion throughout this campaign and, without her support, this victory would not have been possible."

"To my staff, and particularly to my Campaign Manager, Greta Hunter, you are simply the best. This victory is as much for you as it is for us. I have appreciated all of your support through every campaign we have waged together and I am deeply thankful for your ongoing brilliance."

"Now, we have much to accomplish in the days ahead. I want you all to enjoy this moment. For me, I'm now going to retire and go to bed. I can tell you this, however; I will fall asleep with a big smile on my face. Good night and God bless you all."

His private phone rang as soon as he entered the room with Dorothy and Jake. The words were brief but very meaningful. "Congratulations, my dear friend, I wish you the very best". The line went dead but he was well aware of who was on the other end.

# CHAPTER 23

## MIDWAY

**Midway Island, North Pacific Ocean**
**July 4, 2012**

His plane was on final approach to Midway Island. This was his fifth trip he had made, each on his own nickel. It was all to make sure the trips drew no attention from anyone. He wanted as little fanfare as possible.

As usual, Jake had cleared the way for his first meetings and, in fact, attended the first two until the relationship was firmly established.

He was amazed how time and time again that relationships and trust trumped intelligence and brilliance. Without the relationship, these meetings would simply not have been possible.

Midway Island or Midway Atoll is a 2.4 square mile piece of land located in the North Pacific Ocean. It is near the northwestern end of the Hawaiian Archipelago, about one third of the way between Honolulu and Tokyo.

Midway Island is an unorganized, unincorporated territory of the United States. Midway as its name suggests, lies nearly halfway between North America and Asia. It was the perfect meeting place.

Both men were aware that Midway was best known as the location of the Battle of Midway fought on June 4th through the 6th of 1942. In the battle, the US Navy defeated a Japanese attack against the Midway Islands, marking a turning point of the war in the Pacific Theater.

It was so appropriate, as the results of these meetings could mean the turning point in the financial crisis that the United States currently faced. The Presidential swearing in would occur in less than six months and the campaign's final push focused on the financial crisis which made these meetings even more significant.

The United Airlines jet landed on time. There was no driver waiting, in fact, there were very few people around. There were two dusty cabs waiting at the airport. Not many cabs were needed to cover the island since it only has 20 miles of roads.

He had one carry-on bag and threw it in the back seat of the first cab. He told the driver he would like to be taken to 1375 Ocean Front Road.

1375 Ocean Front Road was a typical island residence. It had four bedrooms, four baths and a great front porch that faced the ocean.

He paid the cab driver and waved to the man sitting on the front porch drinking a beer. Once in the house he threw his bag in his room, grabbed a beer and joined his friend on the front porch.

They were getting very close to a final plan and figured that at least two additional meetings would be required, but this one was very important as it had to do with the people who would feel the impact of the plan.

Phat Phing greeted Mac Foster with a warm bear hug. Both men had much in common. Each was heavily relied on by their respective bosses. Each had the total trust of their bosses and both were exceptionally smart and politically savvy.

Neither of their bosses was aware of the nature of their meetings or even that they had met. It was by design, both wanted to make sure that their plan would work before they brought it to the President of the People Republic of China and the Senior Senator from Oregon, who appeared about to be the next President of the United States. The US election was coming up fast. If the Senior Senator from Oregon was elected President he would be briefed. If he was not elected, both men had agreed to forget the idea all together.

They had settled on a price. It was $13 trillion to be paid over a 5 year period. The payment would be all cash.

Today's meeting was focused on the people impacted. Hawaii had 1.3 million American citizens living on the island chain. The agreement that the men had been working on would have a direct impact on all of them when the United States completed its sale of the Hawaiian Islands to China.

Both knew if the word leaked out on either side, the deal would surely be impossible to complete. For that reason there were only three people aware of the nature of their discussions, the two of them and Jake.

They both new that when the transaction was complete that China would nationalize the island and begin to govern in the same way they govern the rest of their country today. It was impossible to relocate the population and to take the land, which was rightfully theirs, under US law, would also be practically impossible.

It was a complicated problem, but they both knew that the overriding benefit of the transaction to each country outweighed these issues. China would have the strategic military position it wanted to control the vast majority of the Pacific Region and the United States would solve, in one transaction, its debt problem and would be free to grow and prosper once again.

Politically, Little Mac knew that there needed to be something that would appeal to those living on the islands. Something that would make them think twice about whether this was a bad decision or not.

Phat knew that he needed the population to see this in a positive way in order to insure order. He also knew that China looked at things long term. What the deal looked like on the surface or, for that matter, over the next 25 years, was unimportant. Phat knew that in 50 years this transaction would be viewed as brilliant and that the Islands, as one viewed them today, would look totally different.

As they sat on the porch finishing their beer, two gooney birds came in for a landing on their front lawn. Both men laughed as the birds crash landed and rolled over a few times before righting themselves up. Neither of the men wanted to see their project crash land.

Gooney birds are the local name given to Albatrosses which are large seabirds that are highly efficient in the air, but just haven't mastered the art of landing. They are found in the North Pacific but are absent from the North Atlantic. They should be named the National Bird of Midway because they are all over the place. They feed on squid, fish, and krill by scavenging, surface seizing or diving.

They met alone for two days and came up with the following framework for the deal.

1. The purchase price would be $13 trillion. All payments will be made in cash to the United States Treasury over a 5 year period.

2. The sale agreement would take the form of a treaty signed between the President of the People's Republic of China and the President of the United States of America. Both understood that a treaty was a formal contract or agreement negotiated between countries. It would need ratification by both countries to become reality. It was not uncommon to see a treaty used as a part of an international trade agreement so it seemed appropriate to both Phat and Little Mac.

3. The treaty would need to be ratified by the Politburo in China as well as the Senate of the United States of America.

4. Once approved, the United States would have three years to vacate all military facilities on the Islands.

5. The citizens of the Hawaiian Islands would all be provided with dual citizenship. They would hold two passports, one from the United States and the other from China.

6. Individual property ownership will be honored by

China and terms of ownership will not change. When a property is put up for sale, the Chinese government will have the right of first refusal to purchase it from the owner at the current appraised value.

7. All elected United States Government Officials must resign when the sale is finalized. The Chinese Government will then assume the leadership of the Islands.

8. Both men also agreed that if they were successful and both Presidents signed the treaty they would coordinate the press release information together. Neither would announce without the other and both would approve each other's press release.

9. The United States would tender a $10,000 payment to every U.S. citizen living on, or who owned property, in the Hawaiian Islands.

Both men understood the magnitude of the proposals they were considering. For China, the motivation was simply power and strategic advantage in the Pacific Theater.

For the United States, it was economic survival and a chance to strengthen its entire financial base – almost a reset for the next half century.

Little Mac had studied this issue in detail. He was well aware that the debt level of the United States was calculated as a percent of the total country's production, or the Gross Domestic Product. The United States total economic output was $14.6 trillion in 2010. That meant that the National debt had reached 90% of the GDP this was up from 51% in 1988.

Interest on the debt was $383 billion in Fiscal 2010, down from its peak of $451 Billion in Fiscal Year 2008, thanks to lower interest rates only.

The most recent budget forecast showed the budget deficit of $1.3 trillion.

Mac was well aware that government debt was the result of an accumulation of budget deficits. Year after year, the government cut taxes and increased spending. In the short run, the economy and voters benefited from deficit spending. In the long term it would bankrupt the country.

Little Mac had estimated that over the next 20 years, the Social Security fund loans must be paid back as the baby boomers retire. Since this money had already been spent, resources need to be identified to repay this loan. This was the resource the government of the United States needed. It was the answer to this national problem.

The two days ended with both men, shaking hands and with the agreement that, the next time, they would meet would be immediately after the U.S. Presidential election if Senator Gavin won.

They headed for the small airport on Midway Island. One plane headed East. The other headed West.

**************************

## Washington, D.C.
## 2013

In November of 2012, the United States elected Senator Bruce Gavin to be the 45th President of the United States. Senator Gavin would be inaugurated in January of 2013. Between the election which occurred on November 6th, and his inauguration, he would begin to appoint his cabinet and his staff. Phat and Little Mac agreed to meet over the Christmas holidays and between now and inauguration both would brief their bosses.

As everyone knew, The President Elect's first appointment was that of his Chief of Staff. It was no surprise when Greta Hunter was named to that appointment. She named as her assistant none other than Jake Rappaho.

In late November of 2012, Mac asked for an appointment with the President Elect. He had coordinated the timing of his visit with Phat so both World Leaders would get the confidential message at the same time.

Little Mac approached Greta and asked for a two hour

audience with the President. He explained that the matter was of great importance and he wanted Greta and Jake to be present as well. The meeting would take place in the Senator's Office, from 4:00 PM to 6:00 PM. The Senator's evening was open so he could hang around in case the conversation spilled over the allotted time.

After the greetings it was obvious that Mac was very serious and on edge. No one in the room, except Jake, knew what would happen next. Bruce gave him the floor.

"Senator", Mac said, "over the course of the past two years I have explored a subject in detail that could have huge significance to the country. I have done this unilaterally, at my own expense, and on my own time. I did so as to maintain a low profile and not involve the United States Government in any aspect of my actions." Bruce looked puzzled; he had known Mac for many years and usually could read him, however, on this occasion nothing came to mind that would fit Mac's seriousness.

Mac continued, "thanks to Jake and his contacts and skills, I have made a new friend who you know. His name is Phat Phing and he is currently the Vice President of the People's Republic of China." Bruce acknowledged that he knew Phat and his boss Woo Wong very well.

The President Elect was, however, still in the dark and the normally brilliant Greta Hunter did not have a clue what was coming next.

Mac continued, "Over the course of five very secret meetings he and I developed a plan that will work well for both of our countries." Both the President and his Chief of Staff now were focused on Mac's every word.

"In a nutshell, Senator, we have worked out the framework for you, as President of the United States, to sign a treaty with China that would provide the United States Treasury with $13 trillion in cash in return for your agreement to sell the Hawaiian Islands to China."

Both the President and his Chief of Staff were totally shocked and for a moment could not say a word. Finally, the President said, "Holy shit Mac! Who else knows about this crazy idea?"

"Mr. President, the only people that know, are those in this room plus effective two hours ago, Woo Wong."

Greta was still in shock. "Mac, you are either fucking crazy or beyond brilliant. I'm not sure which, but I know one thing, I want to understand what was behind your thinking, and what would the terms of the deal be if it moves forward?"

"This could become the biggest load of shit to hit the biggest fan ever", Bruce said as he loosened his tie, sat back in his chair and said, "I'm over the shock. Tell me what you and Phat worked out. We got over a million American citizens living in the Islands. I can't imagine the reaction when this leaks out. What the fuck happens to them?"

Mac then began to explain the points he and Phat had developed.

"First let me start with communications to address your last point Senator. Phat and I both understand the magnitude of the proposal we are asking you and President Wong to consider. If at some point in the future a treaty is signed by both of you, we have agreed that we would coordinate the press release information together. Neither country would announce without the other, and both would approve each other's press release in advance of the coordinated release of information. So, there will be no leaks."

"Shit, there's always a leak...," Bruce interjected, but Mac held up his hand to stifle descent. "Let me explain it all first, then we'll talk."

The terms are not that complicated and we believe we have considered most major issues. Obviously, a trade of this significance would dwarf that of the Louisiana Purchase but it would be along the same lines. Here are the terms.

1. The purchase price would be $13 trillion paid over a 5 year period.
2. The sale agreement would take the form of a treaty signed between the President of the People's

Republic of China and the President of the United States of America.

3. The United States would have three years to vacate all military facilities on the Islands.
4. The American citizens of the Hawaiian Islands would all be provided with dual citizenship.
5. Individual property ownership will be honored by China and the terms of ownership will not change. When a property is put up for sale the Chinese government will have the right of first refusal to purchase it from the owner at the current appraised value. If the Government of China chooses not to make an offer then the open market will prevail and property will change hands like it does today.
6. All elected United States Government Officials will resign when the sale is finalized. The Chinese Government will then assume the leadership of the Islands.
7. All U.S. citizens currently living in the Islands and those who own property, will receive a payment of $10,000 each, from by the U.S. Government.

Now to Greta's question. Why do this? I don't have to go through the economic problems of the United States, nor do I have to explain to this group the interest payments accruing on the National debt daily. The debt has now reached $15 trillion and the interest on that date is approximately $400 billion.

Simply stated, this transaction will solve the National debt issue, it will enable us to fund all of the entitlement programs that are going under including Social Security and Medicare, and it will free up funds to service the needs and desires of virtually every organization that now begs the government for funds.

What about the military point of view? Yes, we lose a strategic position in the Pacific Ocean. We'll never have another traditional war like World War II. If we have one, it will be over without the use of sea power. China knows that as well but this purchase would give them the power they want to control the Pacific Theater and that would mean power over just about every thing in the Far East including Japan. In view of modern technology, nobody can raise the spectre of national security against us. They'll try, but that argument just doesn't hold water."

The discussion went nearly four full hours. Finally, the President Elect looked at Mac and asked. "So, what's the next step in this process?"

"Senator, I anticipate I will need to meet with Phat on two more occasions; the first to provide him with a draft of the treaty agreement. This will occur over Christmas. The second to coordinate your meeting with President Woo and to finalize the press announcements. This will occur sometime after your inauguration."

"With your permission, I will need to confidentially engage the services of John Swift. John has been with us since the beginning, knows how to keep his mouth shut and can do the draft without assistance from anyone else on his staff."

The President Elect looked tired but energized. "No one should do anything or talk to anyone about this subject without my approval. He turned to Mac and said, "I need to think about this for a day or two and then I will get back to you directly."

"Greta, will you arrange a private confidential call for me with my friend Woo Wong in the next couple of days."

With that Bruce left the room. Jake just smiled and said "Mac, you did it again. You blew his mind and he had no idea." Greta agreed. "Mac, you are one smart Jose. You have just changed the future course of America.

# CHAPTER 24

## THE TREATY

**Portland, OR**
**2013**

It was 11:30 PM. Jake and the President left the Sturgis Cigar Bar and began the short walk to the President's highrise condominium in the middle of the Pearl District. It was two short blocks from the Sturgis. Neither spoke a word. Chet walked in front of the two and Josh followed behind them. The routine was always the same. Just before they reached the building the President asked Jake, "What did she decide to do?" Jake responded, "She will be at the appointed place at 7:00 AM tomorrow. She will meet us on arrival." "Good", the President said.

Chet reached the building first and went directly upstairs checking everything out before the President and Jake entered. Once inside they took the elevator to the top floor where Jake and the President entered the suite. Josh and Chet remained outside. They would trade off stations outside the door all night. Jake would cover from inside.

Tomorrow was the Fourth of July and the Nation's birthday. After tomorrow, the Fourth of July might be known as the Nation's "Rebirth Day".

The President went directly to his room and left word with Jake to make sure he was up by 6:00 AM. Jake nodded as he had done so many times in the past.

There was so much on the President's mind. Tomorrow was a major day in, not only his life but, the history of the United States. His personal life was also in major turmoil and those thoughts were with him as well.

He told Mayor Bucky Meyers tonight at the Sturgis, that this would be the last of their entertaining flings together. He talked about Patrick and their relationship and also told the Mayor that he knew now that he and Dorothy were through. Those matters he would deal with in time but now was not the time.

The mayor completely understood. He was gay, had had many one night stands, and most, if not all, came to an abrupt end. He knew that he and the President would remain good friends but that would be the extent of it from this point forward.

Air Force One was parked on the East runway at Portland International Airport. It would remain parked there until July 5th, at which time it would fly directly to Honolulu, Hawaii, arriving shortly before 10:00 AM.

The President would not be aboard that flight but would meet it in Hawaii.

At the far west end of the airport was a new Dasvinit Falcon 7X Private Luxury Plane. The plane was worth $50 million. The plane could carry eight passengers and four crew. It was capable of maintaining a speed of 900 kilometers per hour and could fly from London to Tokyo non-stop. The passenger plane was adapted from the fighter aircraft designed and built by Dassault. The crew manning the Falcon 7X were all members of the United States Air Force. All were in civilian clothes.

At exactly 7:30 AM, the limousine pulled up to the door of the Falcon 7X and four people walked over to the short flight of stairs. The four were in the plane in a matter of seconds. Josh went first, followed by Jake, the President, and then Chet.

Once inside, they were greeted by a very special group of people.

Seated in the plane was the President's Chief of Staff, Greta Hunter. Sitting next to Greta was Mac Foster, the newly appointed U.S. Secretary of State. Next to Little Mac was John

Swift who was now U.S. Attorney General and the former Head of Legal Affairs for the successful Presidential campaign of Bruce Gavin.

In the final seat was the President's guest of honor. Her name was Ming Tai. Ming was a close friend of the President and was his age. She had attended USF with him and had maintained her beauty throughout the years. She had never married but had maintained a very full and rewarding life in San Francisco. The only one on board who knew the reason for Ming's invitation was Jake, and as usual, he didn't share anything with anyone.

The President greeted each member of the group and thanked them for being with him on the eve of such an important occasion. When he came to Ming, he gave her a very long, personal hug. "You look beautiful" he said, "I am so pleased that you were willing to make this trip with us. I realize it may be difficult but I believe that your effort will be worth your while."

The plane lifted off the Portland tarmac and headed directly east for Midway Island.

The President sat next to Little Mac on the first leg of the trip. Little Mac filled him in on his final two meetings with Phat Phing. Both meetings had gone exceptionally well. The Treaty had been finalized and was ready for signature.

Mac explained that John Swift had been through it over 100 times, as have the Chinese attorneys that work for Woo Wong. All are in agreement that it is a well drafted Treaty, but whether it could gain the approval of the US Senate and China's Politburo remained to be seen.

The President then shifted seats to join Greta Hunter. Greta explained that the two Congressmen from Hawaii, as well as the two U.S. Senators from Hawaii, and Hawaii's Governer, would meet them on Airforce One at 10:00 AM tomorrow. Greta told the President that they would be joined by the Speaker of the House of Representatives and the Minority Leader of the Senate.

Each has been told that they should plan to accompany the President on his return trip to Washington. They had no idea what the subject matter was but each was told that the meeting couldn't be missed for any reason.

Greta indicated that their attendance on board Air Force One would mean that the President would have a totally captive audience. It also meant that no one would have the opportunity to contact anyone until the plane lands in Washington.

Greta said that a joint press release had been drafted, and agreed to, by both the United States and the People's Republic of China. The joint press release will be issued shortly before the plane lands in Washington, D.C.

Mac, Greta and John Swift would answer all questions posed by the group. This would follow the President's address to the assembled group.

On their return in Hawaii, the group would board Air Force One. Ming would leave the group at that point and be flown from Hawaii to San Francisco on a private jet. Greta explained, "Ming has been briefed and has committed to total silence in honor of President Woo and yourself, Mr. President." "She can be trusted", the President said.

Greta then briefed the President on his schedule today. He would meet alone with Woo Wong at 3:00 PM. They would be joined by Little Mac and Phat Phing at 4:00 PM. The four would be joined by their legal representatives at 4:30 PM. The Treaty signing would be at 5:00 PM.

"Great" said the President. Jake, Phat and President Wong would sleep at the Ocean Front home. Security would be provided by the U.S. Air Force, as well as the two Secret Service Agents who accompanied the President. The rest of the party would stay at a local island hotel.

Following the Treaty signing, there would be a cocktail hour, followed by an informal catered dinner of fresh island seafood. Greta explained that Ming would be taken to an island hotel to freshen up and then would be driven to the house on Ocean Front, arriving at 5:30 PM.

The group would fly off the island at 8:30 AM on the morning of July 5th. They would arrive in Honolulu in time to meet their invited guests on Air Force One at 10:00 AM.

The plane touched down on Midway Island at 2:00 PM. Ming was driven to a local hotel and the others were driven to the house on Ocean Front. They arrived at 2:45 PM. Phat and President Wong were waiting for them on the front porch.

President Wong greeted President Gavin with the warmest of hugs. "It is good to see you again my friend. You bring back so many great memories of our days at USF together."

The President shook Phat's hand and said, "Phat, it has been a long time. Who would have thought we would be changing the world. It is a pleasure to see you again."

The Presidents were then directed to the makeshift conference room where they would have a full hour alone to discuss the Treaty and to catch up on old times. No one in the room had any idea what they planned to discuss alone, and neither of them would ever share with their staff what their discussions had touched on.

At 4:00 PM sharp, Phat and Little Mac entered the room. They were there to take the Presidents through the eight major points contained in the Treaty document. Phat would explain the first four and Little Mac the last four.

Phat began, "there are nine major policy points contained in the Treaty you have agreed to sign. Mac has already taken you through all of them. Do you have any questions?"

Neither President had any questions as they had been through each of the points so many times that they could picture every word, even as they slept.

At exactly 4:30 PM, the four were joined by the other critical staff that had accompanied each President to the meeting. President Wong and Phat both hugged Jake. They went back a long way together and both had very positive feelings about the six foot seven inch Indian. The other critical staff were introduced to each other and to the respective Presidents.

At exactly 5:00 PM on July 4th, on Midway Island, in a makeshift conference room, in the house on Ocean Front Drive, a Treaty of historic proportions was signed by both Presidents.

Once the official signatures were in place on the numerous

documents required, the Presidents exchanged pens, stood, and shook hands. The assembled group on both sides began to clap their hands. Phat and Little Mac hugged each other.

The Presidents retired to the front porch overlooking the ocean. Each sat in an oversized chair and carried on an easy conversation. Bruce Gavin then looked at Woo Wong and said "Mr. President, I have one last surprise for you on this most special occasion."

As he finished the word "occasion", a black limousine stopped in front of the house. From it appeared a beautiful, middle aged women, dressed in traditional Chinese formal attire. The red silk glistened in the sun as she made her way to the front porch.

Woo Wong could not believe his eyes. Standing before him was the one woman, besides his mother, that he had allowed himself to love.

When she reached the front porch, Ming Tai bowed slightly, looked into Woo's eyes, and with tears in her eyes said "It is very, very good to see you again Mr. President."

The surprise was overwhelming to President Wong. He was completely at a loss? Would it be appropriate to hug her, hold her, or even kiss her? He was in such a state of shock he simply could not respond.

Then, in one joyful moment, he reached out to her and hugged her for what seemed like an eternity to the assembled group watching.

Woo and Ming did not stop talking to each other until 3:00 in the morning. It was obvious that time and distance hadn't diminished their love for one another. They tried to make up for thirty years in a matter of just a few hours. No one ever discussed what went on between them but at 3:00 AM, they held each other for one last time and Woo kissed her goodbye. Ming then turned, walked to the waiting driver, waved to Woo, and then was driven off. She did not know if she would ever see Woo again. The rules of their relationship had not changed, nor could they.

At exactly 8:30 AM on July 5<sup>th</sup>, the private jet took off, headed directly east for Honolulu, Hawaii.

# CHAPTER 25

## CHAOS

**Honolulu, Hawaii**
**2013**

At exactly 10:00 AM, the President boarded Air Force One at the Honolulu International Airport.

He had just said goodbye to Ming Tai as she boarded a specially chartered jet that would take her home to San Francisco. There was no need for a long conversation. The President was right, it was all worth the effort. All she said to him was "thanks Bruce, I will never forget yesterday for as long as I live. It would not have happened without you and I will forever be in your debt." With those words she turned and walked up the short flight of stairs to the waiting plane.

Already seated on the Presidential plane was Leo Lahr, Speaker of the House of Representatives. Sitting next to Lahr was Frank Hanama, the Senate Minority Leader, who also represented Hawaii as its Senior Senator.

Across the aisle from Frank Hanama was Mary Kamehameha, the Governor of Hawaii. In the seat behind Mary was Harry Farmer, the Senate Majority Leader, and sitting next to him was Mike Wong, the Junior Senator from Hawaii. Sitting across from Mike Wong, was Henny Coi, and next to Henny was Elizabeth Chu. Henny and Elizabeth were both congresswomen from Hawaii.

The President's staff made up the balance of the passengers.

The plane door was closed immediately and Air Force One departed, heading for Washington, D.C.

Once airborne, the President stood and addressed the group. "Good Morning, Ladies and Gentleman. I am most appreciative that you were able to join me on my return flight to Washington today. I know this trip has been clouded in mystery for all of you, but I trust you were informed that it was of critical importance that you join me."

"What I am about to tell you will totally shock you, and for the moment, you are going to think that I have totally lost my mind. I can assure you, that's not the case. We have seven hours together before we touch down in Washington. I intend to use every moment of time to answer, as completely as I can, all of your questions."

"To get to the point, I want to share with you a press release that will occur at approximately the same time that we are on final approach to Washington National."

The President proceeded to read the following:

"For Immediate Release from the White House and the President of the United States."

"At exactly 5:00 PM on July 4th, the President of the United States of America and the President of the People's Republic of China, signed a formal Treaty that confirms, that for the price of $13 trillion, the United States has agreed to sell the Hawaiian islands to the People's Republic of China."

There was a noticeable gasp from those seated in the airplane. Each listened to the words that the President had said and sat silently in total disbelief.

The President continued to read. "The agreement is subject to the approval by the nine member Politburo in China, and the Senate of the United States of America."

"The details of the agreement will be disclosed in total to all members of the House and the Senate as well as to the nine members of the Politburo."

"The President of the People's Republic of China, and the President of the United States of America, will personally brief their respective voting bodies."

"In order to insure that there is a measured reaction to this announcement, both Governments will issue a summary of the terms."

"Woo Wong, the President of the People's Republic of China, released the following statement, "We believe that this treaty provides our country with a strategic advantage in the Pacific Theater. We believe that this transaction is in the best interest of our people and we are optimistic that it will receive the approval of the Politburo."

"U.S. President Gavin released this statement, "The cash and debt foregiveness received for this transaction will position the United States of America as one of the strongest and most financially sound Nations in the World. It is an answer to the questions we have had regarding the need to reduce the National Debt and the more than $400 billion we pay in interest on it each and every year. I am optimistic that once all of the facts are provided to the Senate, that they will see the financial benefits that will accrue to the United States which would otherwise not be possible."

"In the U.S., the treaty power is a coordinated effort between the Executive Branch and the Senate. The President may form and negotiate a treaty, but the treaty must be advised and consented to by a two-thirds vote in the Senate. Only after the Senate approves the treaty can the President ratify it. The treaty or legislation does not apply until it has been ratified. "

The President completed the reading of the announcement and opened the floor for discussion. First to speak was Frank Hanama, the Senior Senator from Hawaii and the Senate Majority Leader. "Mr. President, I think you have lost your fucking mind. I cannot possibly support this ridiculous proposal. Every generation of my family has lived on our islands. We have lived under Hawaiian rule and we have been proud of our statehood, and to call ourselves Americans. We simply will not allow anyone to refer to us as Chinese citizens."

Next to speak was the Governor of the State of Hawaii, Mary Kamehameha. "Mr. President, this announcement will paralyze our State. The words contained in the announcement will not stop the fear and panic that will surely follow. I would expect a significant run on all of the banks operating in our State and huge protests to begin immediately. I can envision our students rioting and our peaceful cities destroyed."

The two congresswomen sitting together, Henny Coi and Elizabeth Chu, responded together. "Mr. President, with all due respect, we cannot, and will not, support this action, and we will do everything in our power to see that it goes down in flames."

Last to speak up was Leo Lahr. "Mr. President, I want you to know that at the moment I am pissed off and taken aback, like all of my colleagues on this airplane. I am, however, very worried about the current financial condition of the United States of America and know enough about the bad news it presents to want to listen to the details behind this proposed Treaty."

"Thanks Leo", the President said. "I am not surprised, or shocked, by the reactions that have come from the group thus far. I don't blame you, and if I were in your shoes, I'm sure I would have the same, or similar, feelings. I appreciate the Speakers' points of view and would like to take this opportunity to introduce you to Mac Foster. All of you know Mac and I'm sure you are aware of his keen interest and knowledge of the current financial affairs of the United States. Mac, please brief them in detail regarding the impact that this transaction would have on the current state of affairs."

"Thank you, Mr. President." Mac Foster turned to address the group. With the exception of Leo Lahr, no one from the Hawaiian delegation was listening to the words. Each was trying to cope with what they had just been told. The Hawaiian Islands would be sold to China and each and everyone of them would be out of a job.

The flight from Honolulu, Hawaii, to Washington, D.C. was exactly seven hours and thirty minutes. They had departed Hawaii at 10:00 AM sharp and were expected to arrive in Washington, D.C. at 2:00 AM East Coast Time. At 11:00 PM East Coast time, the press release would be made in accordance with the President's plan. At exactly the same moment in China, which would be 11:00 AM, the same press release would be issued.

******************************

Sally Overman sat in her office in the White House. She had arranged for the release to every major paper in the United States and to the key World News outlets. It was midnight but she was energized. She knew that there would be a non-stop stream of inquires from all over the world. She also knew she would have no sleep for the next two days.

The President had left word with both the House of Representative and the Senate of the United States that he planned a joint address to them on the evening of July 6th. By that time, all of them will know what the subject matter is and the President knew he would have the advantage of knowing what the worldwide reaction had been.

He intended to use the joint session to focus on the numbers and what this transaction would mean for the United States Government. Sally had been working on his talk and had been thoroughly briefed by Little Mac on all financial aspects of the transaction. She had made sure that he would touch on the following subjects of critical importance: the reduction of the National Debt from $15 trillion to $2 trillion; the elimination of the $400 billion of annual interest payments on the debt; the full funding of the Social Security System and a cost of living increase for everyone currently drawing Social Security; the full funding of Medi-Care with an allocation of an annual drug subsidy for all those on the Medi-Care system; the funding of an education fund for all public schools in the U.S.; financial support for State run welfare and food stamp programs.

Sally then had the President focus on the people of Hawaii. He would emphasize the following: they would all continue to be U.S. citizens but they would have the advantage of Chinese citizenship as well; they would all retain the right to their property and would have the ability to sell it at market price should they want to; each citizen would receive from the U.S. Government, a check for $10,000 to be used at their discretion; those who

193

own their own businesses would be allowed to continue to do so. The large financial institutions will have a transition period but ultimately must adopt the same rules U.S. financial institutions are in compliance with today when doing business in China.

Sally already knew that the request for a special joint session of Congress had created quite a stir and a vast rumor mill was operating at full steam. She also knew, however, that all of the rumors were incorrect and when they opened their newspapers with their coffee in the morning that there would no longer be any questions.

At 11:00 PM, Sally triggered the release and double checked with her Chinese counterpart to make sure that both countries were in sync. They were, and the news that would shock the world hit the wires.

*******************************

Little Mac completed his presentation and returned to his seat. The plane was completely silent. Over the course of the next four hours the President met individually with all those present, answered any and all questions, and then returned to his seat.

He managed to sleep for two hours on the flight back and needed the rest given what was ahead.

The headlines were all over the map as the news wires picked up the story. For the most part, they were, however, accurate and most stories followed the facts as presented in the release. The Hawaiian News headline was perhaps the toughest to deal with. The front page of the paper was completely black with the exception of large white letters that spelled out the word **"SACRIFICED"**.

*****************************

Ming Tai would never reveal to anyone what she had learned about the Treaty and the provisions it contained. She did, however, use the information to do one thing; she bought a condominium on Maui two days after her return to San Francisco.

# CHAPTER 26

## THE RUMOR

**Portland, OR**
**2010**

Nora Noitall had been working for the Portland Oregonian newspaper as an investigative reporter over twenty years. One of her biggest stories had involved the Warm Springs Indian Reservation. Her work on that story not only resulted in jail time for the bad guys she uncovered, but also resulted in a huge financial settlement for the Indian Nation.

Nora had had many assignments over her time with the Oregonian but a story emerged in 2010 that her editors wanted her to focus on. In Portland, in that year, an openly gay man had run for the office of Mayor of Portland. His name was Bucky Meyers and he had successfully won the election. It was also during this year that a Federal Judge in San Francisco ruled that Proposition 8, which prohibited gays from marrying, was overturned and deemed unconstitutional.

The editors of the Oregonian assigned Nora to dig into this as a story and to learn whatever she could about the impact this ruling might have on the citizens of Portland.

As she contemplated the story, and her approach, she contacted Jack Samuels, her friend, and photographer, that had helped her so much with the Indian stories.

Nora knew nothing about this issue, nor did she know anything about the gay population in Oregon. Now would be the time to investigate this, weave the Mayor into it and, who knows, uncover a side of the State that few, if any, people even talked about.

She began to do her research. In November of 2008, California's Proposition 8 contained the clause "Only marriage between a man and a woman" is valid or recognized in California. The vote was 5,387,939 to 4,883,460 in favor of passage. That translates to 52.5% for and 47.5% against.

It didn't take long for Nora to learn that this was not a simple issue. The effect of the vote was far reaching and long lasting. There were many sides of the issues but those who were for the Proposition used a variety of tactics that seemed to work with the California population. They made it clear, from their point of view, that unless Proposition 8 passes, all of the school districts will be required to teach children in grades K-12 that same sex marriage is equal in every way to traditional marriage. They also made sure that people understood that churches could have their tax exempt status challenged or revoked if they publicly oppose same sex marriage or refuse to allow same sex marriage ceremonies in their religious building that were open to the public.

Those who favored it also played the adoption card by stating that adoption agencies will be forced to place children with same sex couples regardless of an agency's policies. Additionally, they stated that religions that sponsor private schools with married student housing may be required to provide housing for same sex couples, even if counter to church doctrine, or risk lawsuits over tax exemptions and related benefits. Lastly, it was clear that those who supported Proposition 8 indicated that everyone will pay. Changing the definition of marriage will generate a flood of lawsuits which will inflict heavy legal costs upon those sued and upon business customers.

It was pretty clear to Nora that the campaign had worked. The campaign for and against Proposition 8 raised $39.9 million and $43.3 million respectively, becoming the highest funded campaign on any state ballot and surpassing every campaign in the country in spending except the Presidential contest.

Opposition to Prop 8 was led by the organization "Equality for All." Many notable figures had lined up on both sides of the issue but it was clear that those opposed to Prop 8 simply believed that no person or group should suffer legal, economic, or administrative discrimination.

Then, on August 5, 2010, Chief U.S. District Justice, Vaughn Walker, struck down California's ban on same sex marriage, handing gay rights advocates a historic and invigorating victory. Everyone knew then that this was not the last of this issue. Immediate appeals were expected and the fight was already predicted to end in a showdown at the U.S. Supreme Court.

The issue had also become a political talking point for Bruce Gavin, the Senior Senator from Oregon, who was fighting Barack Obama for the Presidency of the United States. The campaign was just getting underway but Bruce Gavin had come "out of the shoot" on this issue, surprising almost everyone. He supported the rights of gays to marry and also to serve in the Military. No one had any idea if this issue would help or hurt him in the campaign.

President Obama tiptoed around the issue by stating that he personally considered marriage to be between a man and woman, and supported civil unions that confer comparable rights rather than gay marriage.

Nora knew she had a real issue to write about but she still knew nothing about the gay population of the State of Oregon. She wanted to understand it and at the same time, get some idea of the magnitude of the issue in Oregon.

After some thought, she decided to run an article that would focus on the gay and lesbian life in Oregon. She would ask a variety of questions and ask readers to anonymously respond and then she would print the answers for all to see. The questions she formulated were as follows.

- How is gay life in Portland and overall in the State of Oregon?
- What is the tolerance for the gay lifestyle?
- Are there particular places in Oregon where gays congregate?

- What bars and nightclubs do gay's favor?
- How many gays live in the State?
- Are there more men than women or is it about an equal distribution?

In addition, Nora started doing more research on the overall gay population in Portland. She could not get good data but was able to see that in the 2000 census, 8,932 gay or lesbian couples lived in Oregon, an increase over the 1999 Census by 295%. Gay and lesbian single people were not counted, but statistics indicate somewhere between 2% and 10% of the population were gay.

Given the length of time since the 2000 Census, it was clear to Nora that this was a big issue and that the population of gay and lesbian couples and singles had probably increased significantly over the past decade.

The result of her articles painted an interesting picture of gay life in Oregon, and most specifically, in Portland. Given the election results, it was easy to see that the population had a tolerance for this issue clearly above the National population.

Nora and Jack went to work trying to develop a, "Day in the Life of an Oregon Gay Man or Woman". With a top political figure in Portland stating openly that he was gay, the two decided to start following him around, professionally and personally, and documenting as much of his lifestyle that they could witness. The mayor did not know Jack or Nora, so it was an easy assignment.

Jack had done so much work with, and for, Nora that he was able to use his phone to take pictures without anyone, even those sitting with him, would know. This had come in handy on many assignments and he was sure it would on this one as well.

They decided to split the workload. Jack would focus on the gay men's hot spots and Nora on the hot spots for Portland lesbians.

It didn't take long or many conversations for both to learn that Portland is said to be a Mecca for gays and lesbians.

It's the most gay friendly city in the state and one of the most lesbian and gay friendly in the United States.

Nora concentrated on a few selective bars.

The Egyptian Club was Portland's biggest lesbian club. It was open seven nights a week. The E-Room offers a large dance floor, pool tables, bars and karaoke. Once again Nora's pool skills came to play. While she was hit on many times she was able to have a number of interesting conversations about gay life and told those who ask that she was an investigative reporter and was working on a story on California's Proposition 8 and its potential impact on people.

Nora also went to other prominent gay-friendly establishments including the Sturgis Cigar Bar.

On one of his "let's follow the Mayor days," he ended up sitting at a small table in the Sturgis Cigar Bar. The Sturgis Cigar Bar drew a very mixed crowd of gay and straights; men and women all smoking cigars. Jack didn't smoke but, for this occasion, he tried a mild cigar and almost turned green.

Of interest to Jack was an individual who joined the Mayor. It was Bruce Gavin, the Senior Senator from Oregon, who was currently running for the President of the United States. Jack was well aware that the two men knew each other and went back a number of years but he found it a bit strange that in the middle of an election campaign the Mayor and Senator would be socializing, smoking and laughing, in an environment that clearly catered to all people what their race or sexual preference.

Unbeknownst to either, or to the security people in the room, Jack took at least 20 pictures of them. One was of great interest to him when they left their table at the end of the evening and proceeded to the hallway containing the rest room but they didn't enter the door that said "Men Only" on it. Jack wasn't sure but he thought they entered the Sturgis Supply Room located at the end of the hall.

The first time Jack saw them together was in November 2010, but he followed the Senator's schedule and each time he arrived in Portland over the next couple of years he met with the Mayor and sat at the same table.

After watching these meetings, over a two year period, Jack had established a pattern and had pictures of the two entering the Sturgis Supply Room.

All of this was fed back to Nora and detailed records kept of the Senator and Mayor's comings and goings. Neither of them knew where this was going, or if there was even a story here, but both kept digging and were not about to give up.

It was election night and the Senior Senator from Oregon had just been elected the 45th President of the United States. Jack and Nora were at The Benson Hotel like so many others. The President was about to address the audience and the excitement in the room was unbelievable. Jack noticed that the Mayor was present but not paying any attention to the President, it was as though he was running for re-election himself. Off to one side of the room, Nora noticed a Parish Priest that could not take his eyes off of the President. She nudged Jack and said, "Ever seen that guy?"

"Nope, not on my watch."

Nora said, "My stomach tells me that we need to check him out." It just seems strange that a Parish Priest would be so focused on the President. I want to learn everything I can about him.

Nora had met the President Elect years ago when she was working on the Indian Investigation. While she was not sure that he would recognize her today, she was sure that his right hand man, Jake Rappaho, would know her immediately.

It didn't take Nora and Jack long to research Father Patrick O'Callaghan and his long term relationship with the President Elect. Father Patrick was now the District Priest for Washington, D.C. and had been the Senior Senator's roommate at USF. Nora and Jack began to dig in the dirt more and, before long, had the entire history of Father Patrick O'Callaghan.

It didn't take Nora long to send Jack to Washington, D.C. to do a little personal research on Father Patrick and the Senior Senator from Oregon. It was amazing what he was able to

202

develop over the two years between 2010 and the election in 2012.

At the end of the research, Jack and Nora had a very interesting picture to paint of Father Patrick, the Senior Senator, and now, the President Elect and the Mayor of Portland. There was no question there was a relationship but what kind? The only person who could confirm whether there was, was Jake and he simply doesn't talk. That left only the President to confirm or deny.

The election was over, the announcement had just been made that the United States was proposing to sell the Hawaiian Islands to China and there was total chaos everywhere. Nora knew this was not the time to bring this up, but there would be a time shortly, when the subject needed to be broached.

# CHAPTER 27

## THE DIVORCE

**Washington, D.C.**
**2013**

The joint session with Congress had gone well considering the enormity of the issue. The financial ramifications of the Treaty transaction were so significant to the United States Government that few elected officials on either the Democratic or Republican side of the aisle opposed it. The process that the President had outlined to the Hawaiian delegation was now moving forward.

Overall, the reactions had been predictable, although the President had a minimum of twenty death threats since the announcement. The Secret Service staffed up and tried to get on top of the threats.

Hawaii felt hung out to dry and seemed without hope of finding a remedy. Several minor protests had occurred but there was no run on the banks and, for the most part, the rules of the treaty which put money in each citizen's pocket, at a time when they had none, had gradually turned public sentiment towards the President's point of view.

The announcement in China was met with a joyous reaction. The Chinese looked at this as a strategic objective that could never be duplicated. The price was extremely high and would require China to call in some debt from other nations but, overall, they could afford the transaction and felt it was very much in their National interest.

The President did not feel as though he had slept in over a week. His press secretary knew he had not. Everyone was tired with no relief in sight.

Three weeks had passed since the plane flight and the joint session of Congress. Finally, the Administration thought they had their head above water and were ahead of the hostile press.

Nora could not wait any longer. She had purposely delayed her trip in order to allow the President's Hawaiian crisis to blow over. She and Jack had assembled a very significant trail over the past two years and she was sure that, even though he was married, the President was gay and she was going to face him with it.

She booked a flight to Washington, D.C. and an appointment with Jake. She knew Jake well from their joint effort in support of the Warm Springs Indian Reservation. Jake knew she was a straight shooter and liked her very much. However, there was no question that his loyalty was with the President and he would not reveal, under any circumstances, anything he had learned about the President over the past years.

Her appointment was scheduled for a Wednesday at 10:00 AM with Jake in the White House. Jake had no idea what she wanted or what the nature of her call would be but he liked her very much and would always provide the time to her.

She arrived at the appointed moment. As usual Jake was on time and ready to greet her. They exchanged lots of small talk before Jake said to her Nora, "what do you want to meet about? We are reliving old memories but they are not what brought you here. What's up?"

Nora wasted no time. She laid out a detailed description of the President's last two years, and his relationships with both the Mayor of Portland and Father Patrick O'Callaghan. She also produced pictures that backed up her point every step of the way.

"Jake, I think the President is gay and that he had an affair with the Mayor of Portland and is currently involved with a parish priest in Washington, D.C. If I am right, the people of the United States have the right to know. I plan on informing them."

Jake looked at her for a long time. In his normal Indian manner he remained stoic then said, "Nora, if you feel the President has something to hide then you will have to ask him yourself. I am happy to set up the appointment for you. What he says, I'm sure will be the truth. I will get back to you very soon. Where are you staying in Washington?"

Nora said she was staying at the Grosvenor Plaza Hotel. "Jake, I want to deal with this sooner rather than later. If I cannot meet with the President within the week, then I plan to go public with the story and the pictures. Please let me have access to him."

Jake looked at her and said "I will be back to you shortly." They did not hug or shake hands. It was though a transaction had just occurred that neither wanted to be a part of.

It was 10:00 AM in the morning on Thursday when her hotel phone rang. "Hello, this is Nora." Jake responded, "Nora, this is Jake. I have brought the matter you raised with me to the President's attention. He will be happy to see you on this matter at 2:00 PM this afternoon. I will arrange for your entrance to the White House. The meeting will be in the Oval Office."

As was her custom, Nora was early. She prided herself on always being on time. She did not know if the President would remember her but he was the first State Senator she had ever interviewed on assignment and was very helpful in the resolution of the Warm Springs Indian Investigation. That was then and this was now.

She remembered Bruce Gavin as a very open and straight forward individual that did not pull punches. He had always struck her as an honest man, and she, in fact, had voted for him for President.

Frankly, if he was gay, it didn't matter to her, she would have voted for him anyway.

The President's secretary showed her into the Oval

Office at exactly 2:00 PM. The President was sitting at his desk and rose to greet her. He was as kind as she remembered and gave her the feeling that he had never forgotten their Warm Springs event together.

"Hello Nora, it is so good to see you. Jake was in to see me yesterday and indicated that you wanted to see me. He told me it was important and, knowing it was you, I immediately put you on the calendar."

"Jake did not say much about this meeting. He doesn't say much about anything as you know. He did tell me that you were doing a story on gay and lesbian rights and that you had been following the court events around California's Proposition 8. So you are now here and you have my complete attention."

"Mr. President, first I would like to thank you for seeing me and to congratulate you on your election victory. You are correct. I was assigned by the Editors at the Oregonian to do a complete story on Proposition 8 and its impact on the gay and lesbian population in Oregon. My research began at about the time you began to challenge Mr. Obama for the Presidency. So I have been working on this story for over two years."

"During that time, I have written a number of articles on the gay and lesbian population in Oregon and, specifically, in Portland. As you are aware, Portland elected an openly gay Mayor in 2010 which gave us more fuel for this interesting story."

"In the course of our research, we followed a number of gay men and lesbian women during the course of their days and found that they aren't much different than their heterosexual counterparts. They get up early, they work hard, they go out for drinks when they can afford it, and they live their lives normally."

"During our research, we followed the Mayor of Portland on many occasions. This led us to you and your relationship with him. We knew that you have always been friends and to see the two of you together was not abnormal. What we found, however, is that both of you over the past two years have had private meetings in the Sturgis Cigar Storage Room."

"We then began to research your history. Your USF days, and the days of the San Francisco bath houses, and that led us to Father Patrick O'Callaghan."

"Further investigation linked Father Patrick to you here in Washington, D.C."

"We have enough photos to cover the New York Times for a week but that is not my point here today. I simply have one question for you and only one. Mr. President, are you gay?"

"Nora, you have been good at what you do for a long time and to sit here in this office and deny facts that you have researched would not be my style."

"As you know, I have been married for almost 30 years. I have also wrestled with my sexuality during that entire time. It is true that I had a relationship with the Mayor of Portland. It was, mostly, just "fun one night stands". There was no love, or commitment, just two friends having a good time."

"My relationship with Patrick is much deeper and lasting. To answer your question, I am now prepared to tell the nation that I am gay. I am in love with Patrick, and he is in love with me. I don't know where this will take us in the future but it is true."

"This will surely be the biggest "coming out" story in the past 10 years. I would ask only one thing of you. Please do not release your story before tomorrow morning. I need to call Patrick, and I need to sit down and tell Dorothy. That is all I can ask."

Nora just sat and stared at the President. Finally she said, "You know, Mr. President, you have all of the traits that we need in a man running our country. I voted for you and would again. Your sexual preference means nothing to me. I understand your request, but I am an investigative reporter, and I have an obligation to let the American public know what I have learned. I will release the story tomorrow morning."

With that, the President stood, shook her hand, and said, "I appreciate that Nora."

Once she had left, the President returned to his desk and dialed Patrick's private number.

"Patrick, this is Bruce. As we have known for some time,

the story on our relationship, and the fact that I am gay would eventually come out. It will be released tomorrow morning. This will have an enormous impact on both of us, I think we are now ready, to admit to the world that we are a couple."

"As I have told you in the past, my one night stands with the Mayor of Portland, will also be a part of the story. I wish that this were not to be the case, but it is what it is, and I can't change the past."

Patrick listened to every word Bruce had to say and then said, "Bruce, I love you and look forward to a long life together. I am very sorry that this news will be released in the midst of all of the Hawaii issues. I'm sure that this is one thing you would prefer to have delayed. But as you say, it is what it is, and I am ready to get on with my life. I will resign as a parish priest immediately."

"Tomorrow should be an interesting day for both of us!"

Bruce then buzzed his secretary and asked her to call a 7:00 PM meeting with his original political campaign staff. He said it does not matter what their current title is I want the original staff. Here is the list:

- Greta Hunter
- Mac Foster
- Jake Rappaho
- Sally Overman
- Lilly Langoon
- John Switft
- Pete Bailey
- Gretchen March

The President then left his office and went to his private quarters in the White House. He found Dorothy sitting with Petite Crêpe in the living room watching Oprah.

The President went directly to the television and turned it off, which made Petite Crêpe begin to bark at him.

"I have something very important to tell you that cannot wait until tonight or tomorrow. Today I was paid a visit by an investigative reporter from the Portland Oregonian who asked me a direct question. The question she asked was "Mr. President, are you gay."

Dorothy said "What did you just say Bruce?"

"I said, an investigative reporter from the Portland Oregonian asked me a direct question in my office this afternoon and the question was "Mr. President, are you gay."

"For heaven's sake Bruce, why would she say such a thing?"

"Because Dorothy, the truth is that I am, and I am deeply in love with another man. You know him as our Parish Priest, Father Patrick O'Callaghan."

Dorothy sat stunned and then began to turn red. The fire inside of her was about to burn so hot that her entire body shook.

Dorothy then said, "Do you realize what you have just done to me and my position, not only in the United States, but in the world? You have destroyed me, you have made me appear to be less than adequate, you have kicked dirt in the face of the one who has backed you from the beginning, and without me, you would not be standing here as President today." "I cannot believe that you would do this to me. Screw you and your sick perverted friend." "We both know you have not been there for me in years. But to shame me with this is beyond any hurt you could place on me." "I have disliked you for some time, but now can honestly say I hate you. My image is destroyed. I will leave you now, and I do mean now. You will understand, without hesitation, that I plan to file for immediate divorce, and will tell the normal people, who by the way, are still the majority out there, why. You are one sick dude. However, I do not feel sorry for you in any way."

With that she left the room and slammed the door on her way out. She called her private secretary, told her to pack her things for a long trip, and to get tickets for her to leave for Chicago immediately. After that, she held her little "piece of crap" in her hand and began to cry.

Bruce stood there for a couple of minutes in silence, and

then smiled. A huge weight was finally off his back and the rest of his life stood in front of him…he was also crying.

At 7:00 PM, he addressed the group that helped elect him President of the United States.

"Thank you for coming on such short notice. I have something to tell all of you that cannot wait until tomorrow morning."

"To begin with, I have not been honest with you, or with myself, for a number of years now. For years I have struggled with my own sexuality. I was not sure if I was bisexual, heterosexual, bi-curious or gay. I have experimented with each over the years. Perhaps to be entertained, or perhaps secretly within, I was trying to figure it out."

"For the past two years, I have had a sexual relationship with the Mayor of Portland, Oregon. It was never anything serious, just fun for both of us. During this time, I have also had a relationship with my Parish Priest, Father Patrick O'Callaghan. I have known Patrick since college, and up until now, I have been unable to express to anyone that I am in love with him."

"I know this news is a shock to some of you, and to others, something that needed to be said. For some, it has been an elephant in the room that needed to be recognized."

"I am telling this to you tonight because today I was approached by an investigative reporter from the Portland Oregonian who has been able to uncover my relationships, and past practice. To some extent she is a friend and has agreed not to release her story until the morning."

"I have talked with Patrick, and have told Dorothy the truth. As you can imagine she is pissed off, and in her words, "Out of here." She is filing for divorce immediately."

"Tomorrow will be a most interesting day. I wouldn't be here today without the effort of each of you, and it hurts me deeply to think that my sexual orientation could be the cause of my removal from office, and the destruction of all of your hard efforts."

"You deserved an honest statement from me and I wanted you to have it. I have no idea what tomorrow will hold for me, but I can tell you that for the first time in a long while I feel free and energized for the future."

With that, Bruce turned and left the room. The group did not say or do anything. They just sat there in total silence.

# CHAPTER 28

## THE PRESS RELEASE

The President returned to his office later that evening. He had not given his staff an opportunity to question him when he had met with them earlier in the evening. To some extent he was disappointed in himself for not giving those closest to him the courtesy which they deserved.

Sitting in the middle of his desk was an envelope with **"Mr. President"** written on the outside of it. He opened it and in it was a two line message personally signed by everyone he had brought to the conference room earlier in the evening. It read:

"Mr. President, we are happy for you personally and look forward to supporting you for the next eight years of your presidency. Our support will never waver".

For weeks the headlines had all been focused on Hawaii and the President's plan to sell the island chain to the Chinese Government. The treaty approval process had been painstakingly slow because in the United States the treaty power is a coordinated effort between the Executive branch of the Government and the Senate.

The United States House of Representatives does not vote on the treaty at all but the President had included the House in the joint session to explain it and had met personally with all of the house leaders during the weeks since the announcement. The President knew that he would need all of the support he could muster and he was not about to exclude the House of Representatives.

The President knew from the start that the process would be a tough uphill battle. Consent ratification makes it considerably more difficult than the rules and requirements of other countries. The President and all of the members of the Senate already knew that the nine member Politburo representing the People's Republic of China had approved the transaction within two weeks of the announcement.

The President wanted to follow proper procedure in order to foster as much political support as possible for the treaty approval. As such, he had submitted it along with an accompanying resolution of ratification or accession.

He also kept his friend Woo Wong informed every step of the way.

He was, therefore, very pleased when Greta informed him earlier in the day that the treaty and resolution would receive favorable support from the Senate Foreign Relations Committee. The vote by the Committee was 65% in favor.

That left it to the U.S Senate. The Senate was now debating the issue. The main opposition seemed to come from the Hawaiian delegation. The financial impact of this decision on the United States was so compelling that many seemed ready to sacrifice the Hawaiian Islands and their people in order to financially save the rest of the country from ruin.

The President had thought many times about the U.S. political process and politicians in general. If there was something in it for them, and it would buy votes, then they flocked to it like lemmings jumping off a cliff. This was one of those issues. Too many people would not want to worry about the sacrifice of 1.2 million citizens. It was a huge shame, but, unfortunately, a necessary one.

Politics was brutal and the President was about to find out just how brutal when the next story hit.

No one except the President and his staff expected the daily dose of the Hawaiian headlines and stories to totally disappear but they did.

When the story hit the next day, everyone was surprised and most people were absolutely flabbergasted and in total disbelief.

The New York Times Headline said:

**OUR PRESIDENT IS GAY AND IN LOVE WITH A CATHOLIC PRIEST.**

The Washington Post Headline said:

**HE HAS COME OUT OF THE BIGGEST CLOSET IN THE WORLD.**

**U.S. PRESIDENT ADMITS HE IS GAY**

The Portland Oregon Headline said:

**THE PRESIDENT IS GAY. ADMITS RELATIONSHIP WITH PORTLAND'S MAYOR AND CATHOLIC PRIEST**

The President was not surprised and, in many ways, was happy the truth was out on the table for everyone to digest.

The President knew that the issue of his sexuality would be the talk of many for a long time; he was at least pleased that the story, written and credited to Nora Noitall from the Portland Oregonian, was accurate. He did not dispute any of the facts, nor did the Mayor of the City of Portland or Father Patrick O'Callaghan.

All three men were open and honest and answered reporters' questions directly for what seemed like weeks. There were no new revelations. Nora had done her homework and all the facts were written in her article and those that followed it up. As hard has others tried to find more trash to talk about, it just wasn't there.

The strategy, developed by Bruce, Patrick and the Mayor, was to be totally honest, available to answer questions, and be direct with their answers. In retrospect, this was a brilliant way to handle a potentially explosive situation. The strategy included a statement to the citizens of the United States by the President himself and that would be followed shortly thereafter by a National Press Conference that would last until there were no more questions.

This coming out announcement would top all others in history.

Steve Olman, the Senior Republican Senator from Alabama and the head of the Defense of Marriage Coalition, sat in his Capitol Hill Office. It was 7:30 AM and his secretary had just brought him his morning coffee and two newspapers to read. One was the New York Times and the other the Washington Post. He began each day the same by reading both papers, cover to cover.

He opened the folded papers and almost spit his coffee out. The New York Times headline read:

**OUR PRESIDENT IS GAY AND IN LOVE WITH A CATHLOIC PRIEST**

The Washington Post headline said:

**HE HAS COME OUT OF THE BIGGEST CLOSET IN THE WORLD.**

**U.S. PRESIDENT ADMITS HE IS GAY**

Senator Olman had supported Bruce Gavin in the recent election. He did so even though the New Christian Right, which was his base, was opposed to some of the views expressed by Senator Gavin.

The headlines froze him in his tracks. This just can't be true, he thought. I know Dorothy Gavin, she is beautiful, and the two of them have been married for over 30 years. This must be a mistake.

He then began the process of reading every word that Nora Noitall had wrote. The story was very detailed, very long, and contained actual quotes from the President, a Catholic Priest by the name of Father Patrick O'Callaghan, and the Mayor of Portland, Oregon.

When he finished, the Senator felt ill. This was the start of what would be a terrible day.

His phone rang within 15 minutes and did not stop for the next 15 hours.

The first call he received was from the Reverend Bob Moore, who's founding of the Moral Compass was a key step in the formation of the New Christian Right.

Moore began, "Senator, this is Bob Moore. Have you read the headlines in today's paper? "

"Good Morning Bob. I have read the New York Times and the Washington Post this morning but that is the extent of it. Both headlines were shocking."

"Shocking, you bet. I do not have to remind you that you supported this fag in the last election. You did so in spite of absolute objection to his political position regarding gays in the military and the rights of gays to be married. Both were sick positions that could never be supported by those that have elected you."

"You may recall, Senator, that besides abortion, our New Christian Right opposes divorce in general, pornography, premarital sex, and prostitution."

"We have made it very clear that we greatly oppose homosexuality. We have spoken often, and loudly, about our opposition to same sex marriage, same sex civil unions, adoption of children by same sex couples, hate crime legislation that includes homosexuals as a protected group, and the acknowledgement of homosexuals as teachers, soldiers, pastors or politicians."

"If what I have read this morning is true then the candidate that you supported for President is now an admitted fag who supports everything we are against."

"Furthermore, it appears his wife has already said she is divorcing him. Have you thought about the fact that the Supreme Court is at this moment considering whether to listen to the California case regarding Gay Marriage. If the court takes on the case, and if they should rule that marriage between same sex couples is legal, it means we could have a "First Man" in the White House instead of a First Lady. The article says that the President is in love with a queer priest, pardon the redundancy. God forbid if they were allowed to marry. This isn't a "Senator, I told you so", this is rather a "Senator, now that you know you were wrong what are you going to do about it?"

Moore continued, "Senator, do you know how seriously sick this is. Our people are outraged by this news. We demand that you do something about it immediately. We want this guy out, I don't care if he voluntarily resigns or we have to impeach him, but I want him out!"

"We expect an action plan from you and will not wait long for it." With that, Moore hung up.

As the day progressed, the call from Reverend Moore was mild compared to the others.

The Senior Republican members of the House and the Senate were at a loss of where to stand or what action to take. It, however, was clear to all of them that if the American public felt the way that those who called all of them during the week following the announcement, then the American public was not ready to accept a Gay President or a possible First Man in the White House.

It was during this week that the President addressed the people of the United States with a written statement released to all media. This was then followed with the National Press Conference.

The President's National Press Conference was the most heavily attended in history. It was held in the Rose Garden to provide for the crowd. All the media outlets were represented both domestically and internationally. The Press Secretary, Sally Overman, called the group to attention and said that following the President's statement, the President, as promised, would take all questions for up to two hours.

"Members of the press, I'm proud to introduce the President of the United States of America."

"Thank you all for coming today. I first want to state that every word of Nora Noitall's story was accurate and I thank her for the sensitivity she expressed in the telling of it. Yes, I am gay and am finally coming out! What a relief it is."

"Being gay in America is not an easy thing. I grew up confused about my sexuality. I tried very hard to suppress these feelings as just curiosity. I knew the acceptable practice would be for me to think about girls all the time. I tried but I found I enjoyed the company of girls more than I was interested in having sex with them. I watched in silence as friends I knew were harassed and intimidated. I regret that I did not have the courage to stand up for them or to take a public position on the issue."

"In college, I had my first gay sexual encounter. It happened to be with my good friend and my future partner, Patrick O'Callaghan. We were both afraid at the time to admit that it was anything more than just a one time experience. If asked, we both would have adamantly refused to admit that we were gay or bisexual."

"After graduation, I decided that my path was in politics. I felt I could bring solutions to all levels in America. I knew that I had to fit in. I worked hard at keeping an appearance that would be acceptable. I married a woman that I loved. She was also interested in politics and we were a good fit. I don't know if we both ever discussed our political goals but it became clear to us over the years that the best way to effect change was in the White House. We drifted apart through the years, each working on our own agenda."

"My only other gay sexual experience, until recently, was a few occasions with the Mayor of Portland. We both knew it was only a fun outing with no commitment. He was my only partner prior to my reuniting with Patrick. He always advised me to 'Come Out'. He told me that the relief would be unbelievable. I lacked the courage to do so. I now know he was so right."

"I think I have always loved Patrick. We both ran from it; he into the priesthood and me into politics and marriage. So I stand in front of you as a criminal in many American's eyes. My crime is to love someone and, finally, be open about whom I am. In a short time, the U. S. Supreme court will, essentially, rule on the legality of same sex marriage. The morality of same sex marriage is not open for debate. How can it be sinful to follow your heart and your natural tendencies of gender preference? This choice we make as gay people is not an easy one. We put ourselves up for ridicule and discrimination daily. Admittedly, I have chosen to be open only when I didn't have a choice and when my career has already reached its apex. So much braver are those that come out early in life and fight for their rights as American citizens. To them I apologize for my late arrival to the fight."

"I had hoped that a press conference to discuss the Treaty with China would be the one everyone would want to have. We face a financial crisis that can ruin this country and put us on the path to diminished status in just a few more decades. Our debt leverage and continuing growing deficits has brought us and the world to the brink of economic chaos. Our country grew early in our development through the acquisition of territories; some through purchase and some through force. We fought for our independence from Britain and, as a result of that battle, acquired ownership of our 13 colonies. We fueled our growth with the Louisiana Purchase and later the acquisition of Alaska and what is now the States of California and Hawaii. Now, we face a period, where contraction is called for: contraction in our influence overseas, contraction in our spending policies and endowments, and finally, contraction in our habit of borrowing to buy what we clearly can no longer afford. This Treaty with China will resolve most of our financial problems almost over night. However, we have to take this opportunity to make sure that we no longer head down the same path. We, as a nation, must change our ways financially and given the chance, I will make sure we do just that!"

"I now will entertain your many questions."

"Sir, Brian Williams, from NBC, I would like to know if Patrick is going to remain as a priest?"

"No, Patrick is resigning from the priesthood and will teach in a collegiate environment."

"Sir, Audrey Wantit, from the Enquirer, have you ever enjoyed sex with a woman?"

"Boy, Audrey, that is getting right into it, isn't it? Yes, I have and I have enjoyed the closeness that it involves with another person that you feel strongly about. However, the physical aspect of it was much less pleasing."

"Sir, Katie Couric of ABC, do you intend to marry Patrick and have him become the 'First Man' of the White House if the Supreme Court legalizes same sex marriage?"

"Katie, this is way too early for me to be able to answer that question. Patrick and I have professed our love for each other and we both, of course, hope that the Supreme Court finally ends one of the last issues of discrimination in this country. I am happy that we can now pursue our love for each other in a more open, but still discrete fashion. What will happen in the future will depend on how our relationship develops. Also, I think it might be a good idea that I legally end my current marriage before I start talking about another one."

The questions continued in this vein for not two hours but for more than four hours. Gavin never faltered and was direct with all questions. It was a first for any politician. There never was a single question regarding the most significant treaty in the history of the United States.

There was a huge undercurrent flowing throughout Washington, D.C. on this issue.

The Senior Members of the House and the Senate, both Republicans and Democrats, who were opposed to gay marriage and equal rights for gays, met on at least four different occasions following the announcement to discuss the options they had in front of them. All were concerned with the public outrage expressed to them by phone, email and letters.

They concluded after their fourth meeting that they wanted a meeting alone with the President and demanded he give them the time and audience.

They were all caught off guard when he immediately agreed to meet. For another four hours he answered every question they threw at him. He did not waiver from his position, or the facts. It had been a long journey but he told them that he now knew that he is gay and that he is in love with Patrick O'Callaghan, a parish priest in Washington, D.C.

Once the last question was asked, the President said to the assembled group, "should any of you have any additional questions on this issue, I will be happy to answer them either personally or in writing, but now I must attend to the other business that is on our plate, and I mean the upcoming Senate vote on the Hawaiian Islands."

With that, the President turned and left the room. The group just sat in stunned silence.

It was not long after the meeting that the President received a formal letter signed by 50 Congressman and 20 Senators asking for his resignation from the Office of the Presidency of the United States of America.

It took the President less than one hour to formally tell the group in writing that he did not intend to resign and would continue on as President as long as the people of the United States wanted him to do so.

# CHAPTER 29

## IMPEACHMENT

With the President's rejection of the request for his resignation, every right-winged nut on the political right shifted into high gear and began to beat the drums for impeachment. This required a significant amount of research and debate because it was very clear to all of them that the involuntary removal of a sitting President of the United States was extremely rare and difficult.

The conservative members of the House of Representatives would have to move the process forward and, to do so they knew at the outset that they would face an uphill battle. Many were openly doubtful that the President's coming out statement, or sexual preference, would constitute legal grounds for his impeachment.

Article 11.4 of the United States Constitution gives the House of Representatives the sole power to impeach, but it must follow the articles as outlined. Simply stated the article is very clear:

**THE PRESIDENT, VICE PRESIDENT, AND ALL CIVIL OFFICERS OF THE UNITED STATES, SHALL BE REMOVED FROM OFFICE ON IMPEACHMENT FOR, AND CONVICTION OF, TREASON, BRIBERY, OR OTHER HIGH CRIMES AND MISDEMEANORS.**

The conservative House Members knew that there had been much debate in the past about the meaning of these words and they knew that there were three schools of thought on the issue.

The first school of thought interpreted the meaning of the words very liberally, saying an impeachable offense is any event that the majority of the House of Representatives considers to be significant enough at that point in history to remove a sitting President.

The members of the House studying this issue also knew that most legal scholars reject that point of view because it would have the effect of the President serving at the pleasure of Congress.

The second point of view interpreted the words to mean that it would be necessary for a President to have committed an indictable crime in order to be subject to impeachment and removal from office.

The House members could not see how this interpretation could apply to this situation. In fact, they all knew that the Supreme Court was about to consider the possibility of marriage by same sex couples as being constitutional.

The third point of view said that an indictable crime was not required to impeach and remove a President. The proponents of this view focused on the word misdemeanor which did not have a specific criminal connotation to it at the time the Constitution was ratified.

It was the third debate that got the most consideration, but the members of the House of Representatives, who would have to lead this issue, simply couldn't see how it could fit the situation. Many members of the House did not have a problem with the fact the President was gay or straight. They were focused on the real economic issues before the Country. To them, this was all posturing by the crazy religious right.

Senator Harry Farmer, the Senate Majority Leader, met with the conservative members of the House and listened to what he considered to be terrible news. Leo Lahr, Speaker of the House, told the Senator that even the most anti-gay members of the House did not believe that being gay was an impeachable cause.

This brought the Senator to the realization that the House would not be able to help on this issue but he had an idea that might work.

The Senator called a meeting of the "Group of 30". The "Group of 30" was 30 Senators, all from the Southern States, and all supported by the far right of the Republican Party. The meeting focused on the upcoming Senate vote on the sale of Hawaii to China. This required a vote of more than two-thirds of the Senate to approve the sale.

Senator Farmer outlined his plan to the group. Perhaps there is a bit of horse trading to be done here. He knew the President had everything riding on the passage of the Treaty and he knew that the longer the financial crisis was allowed to go unchecked that the citizens of the United States of America would increasingly become disappointed with the new Administration.

The plan was simple. In return for their votes on the Passage of the Hawaiian Treaty, the President would agree to be a one term President and also would agree not to marry while in office. By their estimates, the vote in the Senate would fall short of the two-thirds required by 25 votes. They controlled 30 votes.

While this solution would not appease all of the far right, it would go a long way towards resolving the frustration expressed.

The group was united in this approach and a group of three members were selected to deliver the deal to the President.

The President's appointment secretary received the request from the three Senators and scheduled a meeting with them on a Friday afternoon. The Senate vote on Hawaii was scheduled for the following Tuesday morning.

Jake met with the President alone on Thursday afternoon. As usual he had cut through all of the debates and learned what the real mission of the three Senators was. He told the President that the three had been selected by the "Group of 30" to offer the President a proposition.

In return for their affirmative vote on Hawaii, the President would agree to be a one term President and not to marry while in office.

The President smiled and said "Now that is a different approach. How do they say it on the reservation Jake?"..."I think the term is 'horse trading' Mr. President."

On Friday, at 3:00 PM, the President met with the three Senior Senators. The group was comprised of Harry Farmer, Majority Leader; Steve Olman, Sr. Senator from Alabama; and Mort Wilson, the Sr. Senator from Georgia. The President had known all of them for years and all had supported him in his Presidential bid.

"Good afternoon Senators, welcome to the Oval Office. I'm curious to know what is on your mind so let's get on with it."

"Good afternoon Mr. President", Harry Farmer then said, "Mr. President, as you are aware, we are members of the "Group of 30" which are all Senators with strong support in the South, and the backing of the New Christian Right of our party."

"As you also know, your admission of homosexuality, and your stated love affair with Father Patrick O'Callaghan, has caused an enormous problem with many United States citizens and, particularly with those who identify with the New Christian Right. We all signed the petition asking for your resignation and made it clear to our supporters that we did so. We received your letter of rejection and, thus, are here to propose a deal that we believe will benefit you, as well as those who now oppose you."

"On Tuesday, there will be a vote in the Senate to ratify the treaty you signed with the Chinese Government. You believe that the result of that ratification will go a long ways toward resolving the financial problems our country faces. While we are opposed to decreasing the size of America, we will all vote positive if you agree to the following: You will announce that in light of the division that you're "coming out" has caused, that you will not run for a second term, and secondly, you will agree not to marry while in Office."

The President looked at the Senators and said," what if I do not agree to your terms?"

"Then we will vote against the treaty ratification which will cause your landmark treaty to fail ratification."

"Well Gentlemen, you have given me much to ponder. I will make a decision and deliver it to you personally, here in my office, on Sunday at 3:00 PM. Be sure to be there." With that, the President stood, shook their hands, and opened the door for their departure.

The President then called Greta and asked that Greta, Jake, and Little Mac meet him in his office on Saturday at 9:00 AM.

As he was about to leave the office, he noticed that the mail had been left in his inbox on the side of his desk and on top was an envelope that he knew instantly by the writing, who it was from.

He opened the letter. It was from Dorothy. He had not heard from her directly since she left the White House more than three weeks ago. He had heard indirectly through counsel that she was preparing the divorce papers and would serve him with them shortly.

He began to read the letter.

*Dear Bruce,*

*I have now had three weeks to smolder in the firestorm that you have caused. You have personally ruined my reputation and have embarrassed me beyond comprehension.*

*The divorce papers will be served on you next week. They are very straight forward. I do not want the house in Oregon or the house in Washington. You can have them both. Just stay out of my life for the rest of yours and I will be very happy.*

*I have no idea what will become of your personal life, or your career, but I can honestly tell you that I sincerely hope that you fail miserably with both.*

*You and your gay lover deserve each other and I'm sure will rot in Hell together.*

*This is the last that you will hear from me directly.*

*All correspondence from this point forward will be with my attorney.*

*Sincerely,*

*Dorothy*

The President sat for a moment looking out the window. His thoughts drifted back to the many years he had with Dorothy. Some were very positive, and others not so, but over the 30 years there were probably a lot more good times than bad. He was sorry to have it end like this but it had to end and there was no nice way to let her down considering the circumstances. The President stood and then said to no one, "life must go on and mine will." He turned out the light and left the office, all of the time thinking about his morning's meeting.

# CHAPTER 30

## HORSE TRADING

At exactly 9:00 AM on Saturday Jake, Little Mac, and Greta entered the Oval Office. The President was working at his desk, stood and shook hands with each of them.

"Good Morning. Thanks for coming on such short notice. I'm sure that Jake has told you that I had a visit from three of our most rabidly conservative Senators yesterday. They want to do a bit of horse trading."

"It seems none of them, or those who elected them, are pleased with my sexuality and all that that means. As such, they have decided to use the Hawaiian Island Treaty as their means to remove me from office."

"In return for their votes, and those of the other members in the "Group of 30", to ratify the treaty, they want me to agree to two items. The first is that I will agree to be a one term President, and the second, is to agree not to marry Patrick during my first term."

"I have asked you here for your thoughts on the deal they have proposed."

Greta spoke first, "Mr. President, Jake told us about the deal the "Group of 30" proposed. We have looked at it from a variety of ways and agree that the idea stinks. Now, having said that, we have come up with an idea that we think will work."

"First, we are not sure when the Supreme Court will hear the Proposition 8 case. We believe it will be sometime within the next two years, but we are not even sure of that. We know that even if you and Patrick want to marry, that neither of you will do so unless it is legal beyond a doubt. So, given the fact that we will be at least two thirds of the way through your first term, agreeing not to marry during your first term of office is acceptable."

"The second request, to have you become a lame duck President before you have completed your first year in office, would be a disaster for the country, and would limit your power and influence throughout the world."

"However, we do concede that without their votes, the treaty will fail by a large margin."

"So, we would like you to consider the following counteroffer. After the completion of your second year in office, you will agree to have a nationwide poll taken, by the Gallop organization, to determine your popularity as President of the United States. If the poll reflects a popularity rating that is less than 70% favorable, then you will announce that you will be a one term President. However, if the poll reveals that you have ratings at 70% or higher, then there is no deal and the Republicans will keep the most popular President ever elected in office for another two years. What happens in the second term is what happens."

The President thought a minute and said, "You all feel that the economic impact of the Hawaiian deal with China will be so significant, and fund so many things that are impossible to do today, that it will mean that we can do no wrong, at least in the short term?"

"Yes, Sir, we think the financial implications of the treaty are essential to America and will drive your numbers out of sight with the popular vote. We also believe that there is more of a tolerance for gays and the probability to have legal same sex marriage is greater than at any time."

"Based on our research, and the work that Nora did, we believe that when, not if, the Supreme Court hears the Proposition 8 issue, that it will enable same sex marriage and equality for all."

"So, Mr. President, we think the counteroffer we propose is one that the Senators can't refuse. They get their way and you will not marry during your first term in office. If your popularity meets or exceeds 70% favorable ratings, then, as members of the Republican Party, they will be members of the Party of the most popular President in the history of the United States. They will also have the ability to say that they supported the treaty that saved Social Security, Medicare, reestablished funding for education, and work programs for those unemployed. We are convinced we will have enough money to start the WPA all over again."

"In any event, Mr. President, we believe our counteroffer will work and that it will see you through another four year term after this."

"You all continue to amaze me. I think you have made an excellent suggestion and I will use it with the Senators in my meeting on Sunday." "Now get out of here and go have a great weekend doing something other than working for me."

Jake's car was packed and Andie was waiting for him when he left the White House. It would be a ski weekend for them in Vermont.

Little Mac was headed for a beach weekend in Florida, and Greta was planning to sleep all weekend long.

To all of them, it seemed like they were finally enjoying the eye of the storm.

The President and Patrick would enjoy a quiet evening dinner together, and talk about their future plans.

On Sunday, at the appointed time, the Senators were shown into the Oval Office by the President's secretary. As usual, the President was sitting behind his desk. He stood and greeted the Senators, shaking hands with each one of them.

"Good day Gentleman, please have a seat. You left me on Friday with quite a proposition to consider. I have looked at it from a variety of view points and have a modification to your offer that I believe will meet your requirements." "To make it simple and short, I will agree not to marry Patrick during my first four year term in the White House. Second, I will agree not to run for a second term of office under the following condition:

After I have completed my second year in office, the Republican Party will pay for the Gallop Organization to conduct a popularity poll of me in my capacity as President of the United States. If the poll has a rating that is less than 70% approval then I will announce that I will not run for a second term in office. If the approval rating is higher than 70%, then I will have your support in returning for another attempt to win another four years for the Republican Party."

"It looks to me like this is an opportunity for you to win on a number of fronts. First, there will be no "First Man" in the White House in the near future. Second, if my popularity with the American people is less than 70% favorable after two years, I will agree to not run for a second term. If, however, my approval rating is greater than 70%, then you will be members of the party that has elected, and supported, the most popular President in the history of the United States. Last, by voting in favor of the Hawaiian Treaty, you will be able to say that you supported the greatest financial boost to the country in history, and your vote was key to saving Social Security and Medicare, not to mention, all of the other programs that will be enabled by the money available."

"Gentlemen, in your neck of the woods, I think one would say 'you can have your cake and eat it too'. What do you say?"

The Senators did not speak, their minds were moving at a mile a minute. Finally Senator Haley said, "You have offered us a very interesting proposition that I, for one, can support, and will recommend to the others." The other two Senators did not speak but smiled and nodded their approval. Clearly they felt the poll would never show a 70% approval rating since it has never been close to that in the history of the Gallup Poll.

"Then, gentlemen, if I can take your comments and nodding as an agreement, then I think we have a deal.

"I look forward to a win for all of us on Tuesday's vote.

Thank you for taking the time out of your weekend to discuss this matter."

On Tuesday, the Senate of the United States voted by a 5 vote margin, to ratify the treaty with China to sell the Hawaiian Islands for $13 trillion. The first call the President made on hearing the results was to Woo Wong.

The President's only comment to his good friend was to say "My dear friend, we have a deal."

# CHAPTER 31

## THE GHOST DANCE

**Oregon**
**2013**

The first American Indian Ghost Dance was performed in 1870. The dance proclaimed that the world would soon be destroyed, and then renewed; the dead would be brought back to life, and game animals restored. The dance had many different versions over the years and it meant different things to different tribes.

The Ghost Dance was similar to the Plateau Prophet Dance developed by the Paiute Indians. The Ghost Dance, however, addressed very present conditions of deprivation resulting from white incursion into tribal territories. It spread to California, Oregon, and Idaho.

For the Warm Springs Indian Tribe it reaffirmed the encroachment that they experienced. No better example than the fight over the Deschutes River.

The Ghost Dance also combined with an earlier ceremony which gave thanksgiving to God for food. As a result, the annual renewal of nature took on a cosmic dimension; shamans, or Indian medicine men, reported dreams in which they saw the dead assembled in heaven waiting to return to Earth at some unspecified time in the future. The Warm Springs Indian Tribe anticipated this event and performed the dance at special times of the year, and always at elder's funerals.

Such was the case at this funeral. It was a bright sunny fall day on the Warm Springs Reservation. Over 1,000 people had descended on the reservation that day to pray for the sprit of one such elder.

Sacajawea Rappaho was dead at the age of 92.

Jake learned of her passing by a phone call from Cheetah Rains. Cheetah called him immediately and could not stop crying on the phone. Jake had never heard Cheetah cry, let alone express emotion. Between sobs she said "Jake, your mom passed away this morning. She died in her sleep at the cabin. I am so sorry and so sad for all of us. She was like a mother to me and to hundreds of us that grew up on the Reservation. I wanted you to know immediately."

Jake called the President and Greta, and left immediately for Portland. The drive over to the Reservation took about three hours and Cheetah was at his house when he arrived. Her eyes were as red as they could be. She looked exhausted and, for the first time in his life, she looked frail.

She fell into his arms and started crying again. He just held her tight for what seemed like an hour.

Native American nations do not share a single faith or common practice, however, over the years, a number of observations have been made that they all share certain things in common about sacred services.

- Sacred services are both personal and communal experiences meant to shape the individual.
- All Gods creations are viewed as sacred.
- Nature should be revered, not simply evidence of a creator, but sacred in itself.
- Specific areas, or sites, are important to sacred ceremonies. They are more often a homeland than a shrine or temple.
- All life is an equal part of creation. This view places human beings on the same level as insects or animals.
- Death is a journey to another world.

Such was the belief of the Indian Nation who lived on the

Warm Springs Reservation. Sacajawea Rappaho had begun her journey to another world.

The ceremony would be held at the top of the highest hill overlooking the Deschutes River. Here nature reached to touch the sky and it was here that Sacajawea Rappaho's final resting service would be held. It was the most sacred service of all.

Jake and Cheetah spent the next two weeks planning the service with the Elders of the Warm Springs Nation.

This would be no ordinary service of a simple passing. Sacajawea Rappaho was a known Elder to all Indian Nations. Her long life and wisdom had touched so many people that this would be a service like no other ever seen on Warm Springs Land.

The President of the United States would attend. He would be the first to attend a Native American Indian funeral, which was one more indication of the love and respect that Sacajawea had earned over the period of her life.

The President called his friend, John Thomas, Governor of the State of Oregon, and together they made the decision that all flags on Oregon Federal and State Facilities would be flown at half mast for a period of a week leading up to the funeral.

Nora Noitall made sure that all of Oregon and half of the United States knew who Sacajawea Rappaho was and what her many contributions were to the State of Oregon and to the many Native American Tribes that touched her.

The headline in the Oregonian said: "GREAT TRIBAL LEADER HAS PASSED ON. A PART OF OREGON INDIAN HISTORY IS LOST."

In some Native American funeral practices, relatives of the deceased are subject to strict rules in order to assist their departed on their journey. Personal items are often placed in the coffin. While native beliefs hold that death is not the end of life, sympathy is welcome to help ease the loss of the loved one.

Jake and Cheetah both placed personal items in the coffin of Sacajawea Rappaho.

The day of the funeral came very quickly although it had been two full weeks since she had passed on.

Over 1,000 people attended the ceremony. Representatives from all Indian Tribes from the Midwest to the West coast were in attendance. It seemed like half of the people from Oregon were in attendance, plus the President of the United States and the Director of the Bureau of Indian Affairs.

All Native Americans were in full tribal dress, as were the eight pallbearers that carried Sacajawea to her final resting place on the sacred hill overlooking the Deschutes River. On the front of each side of the coffin were Jake and Cheetah. Both were in full Indian dress. Cheetah was in white buckskin with assorted colorful beads adorning it. Jake was in natural buckskin. He wore a bandana and a simple necklace made of bear claws. Both wore knee length leather moccasins.

With Jake's height, and Cheetah's beauty, the two simply looked the part they had played their entire life. They were Warm Springs Indians, proud of their heritage and of the woman that they now carried to her final resting place. The Tribe elders made up the additional six pallbearers.

The tribal elders were followed by a young Indian brave who led five white horses. He was in full Indian dress and was about 12 years old. He was followed by the last person in the precession. It was a young Indian girl of the same age. She led one single black stallion. The picture of the precession would be one that all in attendance would never forget.

The ceremony was not long. The ghost dance was performed. The Medicine Man from the Warm Spring's Tribe, along with the Tribe Elders, each touched the coffin as if to wish it God speed as it carried Sacajawea on her way to her next life. Smoke was released from a small vase and words were spoken in the Indian dialect that few could understand.

When it was over, the sun was about to set in the West. It had been a wonderful ceremony and one that everyone in attendance would remember forever.

The following day, Jake and Cheetah were on the front

page of the Oregonian, and for that matter, every newspaper in Oregon.

When everyone had left, and all had left their words of loss with Jake and Cheetah, the two returned to Sacajawea's small house. It was the house that Jake had grown up in. It was at the end of a long dusty road. Jake's horse, Hawk, was still there but could no longer be ridden.

They sat on the porch without saying a word.

Almost as if on queue, they left the porch, went into Jake's old bedroom, and made the most passionate love together that they had ever experienced.

It was then, in the small cabin, in his old room with his childhood sweetheart that Jake knew that this was his home and where he would eventually end up. He also knew that his future wife was lying next to him. He would marry Cheetah Rains.

# CHAPTER 32

## THE AFTERMATH

**Washington, D.C.**
**2013**

The vote in the Senate was 72 to 28 in favor of the Treaty with China. With the vote, the Treaty was ratified, and the sale of the island chain could now move forward in accordance with the Treaty document.

This was a major victory for the President, and the cash impact on the United States was stunning.

The stock market soared on the news but the general mood of the country was noticeably mixed. There was no question that everyone who wanted something from the Government now thought it was possible. Yet, there was a sadness in sacrificing their beautiful Hawaii.

The President advised the U.S. Department of Treasury, and the Office of Management and Budget, to revise their four year outlook plans for government spending and to report back to him as soon as possible. The President planned a major address to the American people on the Country's financial outlook, and he wanted to make it sooner rather than later.

Little press attention had been paid to Afghanistan, but the President had not lost sight of his campaign promise. The resistance to pull out was there and not going away easily. Some progress was being made on the pull out issue and the

President made sure that the American people were aware of his position on the issue but there was resistance.

The President found the reaction by the citizens of Hawaii to be the most interesting. The fact that they would all have additional money in their pocket, joint citizenship, and would retain their homes and businesses, had most believing that this wasn't such a bad deal after all. The President, however, knew that the negative reactions would occur once China began to implement their form of Government, but there would be a significant amount of time before that impact hit home. In the meantime, all seemed well in the island chain.

Greta managed the President's life like it was her own. She made sure that there were no mistakes made on any front. She used Jake as a means of sensing issues before the President took positions on them, and made sure that his gay lifestyle was maintained on a low profile.

The President and Patrick's relationship was like a farmer who simply could not give up his old worn shoes. They were totally comfortable together, open and honest in their feelings, but mindful of the President's position.

Patrick gave up his position as a Parish Priest, but was asked to teach religious studies at Georgetown University. The fact that he was gay meant nothing to the University. His classes were packed, with waiting lists to get in.

Patrick maintained a small but comfortable apartment near Georgetown University. The President spent many evenings there for dinner, but, by agreement, did not stay overnight.

Dorothy's divorce request was a slam dunk. It went through faster than butter could melt on a hot knife. Dorothy remained in Chicago and took an active role in her company. She served as Chairman of the Board while her best friend Brit continued to run the company. Dorothy was inseparable from her dog, Petite Crêpe. The dog went with her everywhere and fit nicely in her purse. The President rarely referred to the dog again; but, when he did, he always called it a "pile of crap". Dorothy and Brit fell back into their college routine by rounding up a cadre of men that were always willing to meet their every need. It was purely a physical thing with both of them. Once the need was fulfilled, then that was the end of the relationship. Unfortunately, she would always be branded with the reputation that her sexual appeal couldn't stop her husband from turning gay. While she knew, and the President knew, it had nothing to do with her sexual ability; you couldn't convince many of the people in the United States that that was the case.

The President sold the Georgetown mansion that Dorothy had walked away from. He said nothing to her but, when escrow closed, he sent the $2.5 million check to Dorothy in Chicago. She never responded, and he could have cared less. He used the other $.5 million to fund a scholarship for kids at Marshall High School in Portland. The scholarship was in the name of Rebecca Laceful.

The President maintained the Charbonneau Home as his West Coast residence. He gifted the large three bedroom condominium in the Pearl District to Toni and Mike. They were blown away by the gesture but were in seventh heaven with only a two block walk to the Sturgis Cigar Bar. Toni could not get over the view of the Willamette River and Mount Hood. Every night she sat in her window, rain or shine, and watched the moon rise from the East over Mt. Hood.

The Sturgis Cigar Bar, primarily because of the President, became the most popular bar in Portland. It was packed nightly with a wide range of people young and old, gay and straight. As to race and sex, the place was a natural melting pot. The old storage room was returned to its primary use and now housed mops and brooms where the famous bed once stood.

Toni and Mike made their annual trek to Sturgis on their new Harley, and Toni managed to convince Mike that new leathers each year for the occasion were appropriate. Her pink leather outfit was still her favorite but now she had a lime green one and a turquoise blue one as well. Needless to say, the front of each was cut so low it had truck drivers swerving to stay on the road as they passed them in route to the event.

The President and Patrick made the bar a regular stop on their way from the airport to Charbonneau, and tried to be in

Portland at least once every other month. They were always accompanied by Jake, Josh and Chet.

Nora was promoted to Editor of the Portland Oregonian. She continued to live in her apartment off 23$^{rd}$ and Burnside just above the Pearl District. She did not marry, but continued her on and off relationship with John Thomas. She loved their nights together at the cabin on Mount Hood but did not know if there would be a marriage in her future. Nora became good friends with Patrick and the President, and was included in all social occasions held at the Charbonneau home.

The original staff had all been absorbed in the new Administration. The assignments appointed or approved were as follows.

| | |
|---|---|
| Jebb Bramble | Vice President |
| Greta Hunter | Chief of Staff |
| Jake Rappaho | Special Assistant to the President – Secrete Service Status |
| Mac Foster | Secretary of State |
| Sally Overman | Press Secretary for the Administration |
| Pete Bailey | Secretary to the President and Appointment Secretary |
| Gretchen March | Director of Information Services the White House |
| John Swift | Attorney General of the United States |
| Lilly Langoon | Secretary, Department of Health and Human Services |

The President watched carefully the first step of implementation of the Hawaiian Treaty of 2014. The process was working well, thanks in part to Mac Foster and Phat Phing.

The war in Afghanistan was not winding down, and the process put in place to remove all troops was way off schedule. He did not believe that a withdrawal could be made in the time he had left. There was simply too much opposition.

The President's approval ratings were extremely high, no matter who measured them, which was of significant interest to the Group of 30 who waited patiently for the completion of his second year, and the poll they had been awaiting eagerly.

The Supreme Court had agreed to hear the appeal of the California Proposition 8 matter, which would, if upheld, legalize same sex marriage. Everyone expected the Court to hear the issue before the President completed his first term in office.

There were a few things that the President was saddened by during his first two years in office. Perhaps the most important and personal one to him was the passing of Jake's mother, Sacajawea Rappaho. What a wonderful woman she was. She simply could never be replaced and the Warm Springs Indian Reservation would never be the same without her. The President personally attended her funeral, as did over 1,000 others.

He felt sad about the relationship between Woo Wong and the love of his life, Ming Tai. He knew they may never be together again but hoped that at some point in the future they would figure out a way to continue their love. The President did not know that Ming had purchased a condo on Maui and would have dual citizenship at some point in the future.

The President sat alone in his Oval Office watching as the late winter snow fell in Washington. He was well into his second year. Much had happened and most of it good. The future was difficult to predict. Few knew that his future depended on the Republican Party Poll which would be conducted in January. If the outcome was positive, it would help define where he would go from there. If negative, then he and Patrick would certainly return to Oregon after he completed his first term.

So much depended on the Poll.